REGINALD IN RUSSIA

quotes from REGINALD IN RUSSIA

'Vanessa began to arrive at the conclusion that a husband who added a roving disposition to a settled income was a mixed blessing. It was one thing to go to the end of the world; it was quite another thing to make oneself at home there. Even respectability seemed to lose some of its virtue when one practised it in a tent.'

' "There's always a chance that one of them might turn out depraved and vicious, and then you could disown him. I've heard of that being done."
"But, good gracious, you've got to educate him first. You can't expect a boy to be vicious till he's been to a good school." '

' "No one knows what I suffer from indigestion" was one of her favourite statements, but the lack of knowledge can only have been caused by defective listening; the amount of information available on the subject would have supplied material for a monograph.'

'The brutal directness of the masculine shopper arouses a certain combative derision in the feminine onlooker. A cat that spreads one shrew mouse over the greater part of a long summer afternoon, and then possibly loses him, doubtless feels the same contempt for the terrier who compresses his rat into ten seconds of the strenuous life.'

'He had a stuffed bittern in his study, and knew the names of quite a number of wild flowers, so his aunt had possibly some justification in describing him as a great naturalist . . .'

'He said horrid things about other people in such a charming way that one forgave him for the equally horrid things he said about oneself behind one's back. Hating anything in the way of ill-natured gossip ourselves, we are always grateful to those who do it for us . . .'

'Two against three would have been exciting and possibly unpleasant, one against three promised to be about as amusing as a visit to a dentist. Rollo ordered his carriage for as early as was decently possible, and faced the company with a smile that he imagined the better sort of aristocrat would have worn when mounting to the guillotine.'

'Agnes was fat first and good natured afterwards, those were her guiding principles in life. She was profuse in her sympathy for Dolores, but she hastily devoured the peach, explaining that it would spoil it to divide it; the juice ran out so.'

' "Can any of you recite?"
There were symptoms of a general panic. Dolores was known to recite "Locksley Hall" on the least provocation. There had been occasions when her opening line, "Comrades, leave me here a little," had been taken as a literal injunction by a large section of her hearers.'

REGINALD IN RUSSIA

by

SAKI
(H. H. MUNRO)

ADELAIDE
MICHAEL WALMER
2014

Reginald in Russia first published 1910
This edition first published 2014

by

Michael Walmer
49 Second Street
Gawler South
South Australia 5118

ISBN 978-0-9925234-1-1 paperback

ERRATA

This edition has been prepared utilizing a previous edition; thus errors have been reproduced. On page 67, line 26, for *fair* please read *fare*.

TO

M. V. P.

CONTENTS

" The Baker's Dozen" originally appeared
in " The Journal of the Leinster Regi-
ment." The other sketches have appeared
from time to time in the "Westminster
Gazette." To the Editors of these publi-
cations I am indebted for courteous per-
mission to reproduce the stories in their
present form.

REGINALD IN RUSSIA

R EGINALD sat in a corner of the
Princess's salon and tried to forgive
the furniture, which started out with an
obvious intention of being Louis Quinze, but
relapsed at frequent intervals into Wilhelm II.

He classified the Princess with that distinct
type of woman that looks as if it habitually
went out to feed hens in the rain.

Her name was Olga; she kept what she
hoped and believed to be a fox-terrier, and
professed what she thought were Socialist
opinions. It is not necessary to be called
Olga if you are a Russian Princess; in fact,
Reginald knew quite a number who were
called Vera; but the fox-terrier and the
Socialism are essential.

"The Countess Lomshen keeps a bull-dog,"
said the Princess suddenly. "In England is
it more chic to have a bull-dog than a fox-
terrier?"

Reginald threw his mind back over the canine fashions of the last ten years and gave an evasive answer.

" Do you think her handsome, the Countess Lomshen ? " asked the Princess.

Reginald thought the Countess's complexion suggested an exclusive diet of macaroons and pale sherry. He said so.

"But that cannot be possible," said the Princess triumphantly; " I've seen her eating fish-soup at Donon's."

The Princess always defended a friend's complexion if it was really bad. With her, as with a great many of her sex, charity began at homeliness and did not generally progress much farther.

Reginald withdrew his macaroon and sherry theory, and became interested in a case of miniatures.

"That ? " said the Princess; " that is the old Princess Lorikoff. She lived in Millionaya Street, near the Winter Palace, and was one of the Court ladies of the old Russian school. Her knowledge of people and events was extremely limited; but she used to patronise every one who came in contact with her. There was a story that when she died and left the Millionaya for Heaven she addressed

St. Peter in her formal staccato French : ' Je suis la Princesse Lor-i-koff. Il me donne grand plaisir à faire votre connaissance. Je vous en prie me présenter au Bon Dieu.' St. Peter made the desired introduction, and the Princess addressed le Bon Dieu : ' Je suis la Princesse Lor-i-koff. Il me donne grand plaisir à faire votre connaissance. On a souvent parlé de vous à l'église de la rue Million.' "

" Only the old and the clergy of Established churches know how to be flippant gracefully," commented Reginald ; " which reminds me that in the Anglican Church in a certain foreign capital, which shall be nameless, I was present the other day when one of the junior chaplains was preaching in aid of distressed somethings or other, and he brought a really eloquent passage to a close with the remark, ' The tears of the afflicted, to what shall I liken them—to diamonds ? ' The other junior chaplain, who had been dozing out of professional jealousy, awoke with a start and asked hurriedly, ' Shall I play to diamonds, partner ? ' It didn't improve matters when the senior chaplain remarked dreamily but with painful distinctness, ' Double diamonds.' Every one looked at the preacher, half expecting him to redouble, but he contented himself with scoring what points he could under the circumstances."

"You English are always so frivolous," said the Princess. "In Russia we have too many troubles to permit of our being light-hearted."

Reginald gave a delicate shiver, such as an Italian greyhound might give in contemplating the approach of an ice age of which he personally disapproved, and resigned himself to the inevitable political discussion.

"Nothing that you hear about us in England is true," was the Princess's hopeful beginning.

"I always refused to learn Russian geography at school," observed Reginald; "I was certain some of the names must be wrong."

"Everything is wrong with our system of government," continued the Princess placidly. "The Bureaucrats think only of their pockets, and the people are exploited and plundered in every direction, and everything is mismanaged."

"With us," said Reginald, "a Cabinet usually gets the credit of being depraved and worthless beyond the bounds of human conception by the time it has been in office about four years."

"But if it is a bad Government you can turn it out at the elections," argued the Princess.

"As far as I remember, we generally do," said Reginald.

"But here it is dreadful, every one goes to such extremes. In England you never go to extremes."

"We go to the Albert Hall," explained Reginald.

"There is always a see-saw with us between repression and violence," continued the Princess; "and the pity of it is the people are really not in the least inclined to be anything but peaceable. Nowhere will you find people more good-natured, or family circles where there is more affection."

"There I agree with you," said Reginald. "I know a boy who lives somewhere on the French Quay who is a case in point. His hair curls naturally, especially on Sundays, and he plays bridge well, even for a Russian, which is saying much. I don't think he has any other accomplishments, but his family affection is really of a very high order. When his maternal grandmother died he didn't go as far as to give up bridge altogether, but he declared on nothing but black suits for the next three months. That, I think, was really beautiful."

The Princess was not impressed.

" I think you must be very self-indulgent and live only for amusement," she said, " a life of pleasure-seeking and card-playing and dissipation brings only dissatisfaction. You will find that out some day."

" Oh, I know it turns out that way sometimes," assented Reginald. " Forbidden fizz is often the sweetest."

But the remark was wasted on the Princess, who preferred champagne that had at least a suggestion of dissolved barley-sugar.

" I hope you will come and see me again," she said, in a tone that prevented the hope from becoming too infectious; adding as a happy afterthought, " you must come to stay with us in the country."

Her particular part of the country was a few hundred versts the other side of Tamboff, with some fifteen miles of agrarian disturbance between her and the nearest neighbour. Reginald felt that there is some privacy which should be sacred from intrusion.

THE RETICENCE OF LADY ANNE

E GBERT came into the large, dimly lit drawing-room with the air of a man who is not certain whether he is entering a dovecote or a bomb factory, and is prepared for either eventuality. The little domestic quarrel over the luncheon-table had not been fought to a definite finish, and the question was how far Lady Anne was in a mood to renew or forgo hostilities. Her pose in the arm-chair by the tea-table was rather elaborately rigid; in the gloom of a December afternoon Egbert's pince-nez did not materially help him to discern the expression of her face.

By way of breaking whatever ice might be floating on the surface he made a remark about a dim religious light. He or Lady Anne were accustomed to make that remark between 4.30 and 6 on winter and late autumn evenings; it was a part of their married life. There was no recognised rejoinder to it, and Lady Anne made none.

Don Tarquinio lay astretch on the Persian rug, basking in the firelight with superb indifference to the possible ill-humour of Lady Anne. His pedigree was as flawlessly Persian as the rug, and his ruff was coming into the glory of its second winter. The page-boy, who had Renaissance tendencies, had christened him Don Tarquinio. Left to themselves, Egbert and Lady Anne would unfailingly have called him Fluff, but they were not obstinate.

Egbert poured himself out some tea. As the silence gave no sign of breaking on Lady Anne's initiative, he braced himself for another Yermak effort.

" My remark at lunch had a purely academic application," he announced ; "you seem to put an unnecessarily personal significance into it."

Lady Anne maintained her defensive barrier of silence. The bullfinch lazily filled in the interval with an air from *Iphigénie en Tauride*. Egbert recognised it immediately, because it was the only air the bullfinch whistled, and he had come to them with the reputation for whistling it. Both Egbert and Lady Anne would have preferred something from *The Yeomen of the Guard*, which was their favourite opera. In matters artistic they had a similarity of taste. They leaned towards the honest and explicit in art, a picture, for instance, that told its own story, with generous assistance from its title. A riderless warhorse with harness in obvious disarray, staggering into a courtyard full of pale swooning women, and marginally noted " Bad News," suggested to their minds a distinct interpretation of some military catastrophe. They could see what it was meant to convey, and explain it to friends of duller intelligence.

The silence continued. As a rule Lady Anne's displeasure became articulate and markedly voluble after four minutes of introductory muteness. Egbert seized the milk-jug and poured some of its contents into Don Tarquinio's saucer ; as the saucer was already full to the brim an unsightly overflow was the result. Don Tarquinio looked on with a surprised interest that evanesced into elaborate unconsciousness when he was appealed to by Egbert to come and drink up some of the spilt matter. Don Tarquinio was prepared to play many rôles in life, but a vacuum carpet-cleaner was not one of them.

"Don't you think we're being rather foolish?" said Egbert cheerfully.

If Lady Anne thought so she didn't say so.

"I dare say the fault has been partly on my side," continued Egbert, with evaporating cheerfulness. "After all, I'm only human, you know. You seem to forget that I'm only human."

He insisted on the point, as if there had been unfounded suggestions that he was built on Satyr lines, with goat continuations where the human left off.

The bullfinch recommenced its air from *Iphigénie en Tauride*. Egbert began to feel depressed. Lady Anne was not drinking her tea. Perhaps she was feeling unwell. But when Lady Anne felt unwell she was not wont to be reticent on the subject. "No one knows what I suffer from indigestion" was one of her favourite statements; but the lack of knowledge can only have been caused by defective listening; the amount of information available on the subject would have supplied material for a monograph.

Evidently Lady Anne was not feeling unwell.

Egbert began to think he was being un-
reasonably dealt with ; naturally he began to
make concessions.

" I dare say," he observed, taking as central
a position on the hearth-rug as Don Tarquinio
could be persuaded to concede him, " I may
have been to blame. I am willing, if I can
thereby restore things to a happier standpoint,
to undertake to lead a better life."

He wondered vaguely how it would be
possible. Temptations came to him, in
middle age, tentatively and without insistence,
like a neglected butcher-boy who asks for a
Christmas box in February for no more
hopeful reason than that he didn't get one in
December. He had no more idea of suc-
cumbing to them than he had of purchasing
the fish-knives and fur boas that ladies are
impelled to sacrifice through the medium of
advertisement columns during twelve months
of the year. Still, there was something im-
pressive in this unasked-for renunciation of
possibly latent enormities.

Lady Anne showed no sign of being
impressed.

Egbert looked at her nervously through
his glasses. To get the worst of an argument
with her was no new experience. To get the

worst of a monologue was a humiliating novelty.

"I shall go and dress for dinner," he announced in a voice into which he intended some shade of sternness to creep.

At the door a final access of weakness impelled him to make a further appeal.

"Aren't we being very silly?"

"A fool" was Don Tarquinio's mental comment as the door closed on Egbert's retreat. Then he lifted his velvet forepaws in the air and leapt lightly on to a bookshelf immediately under the bullfinch's cage. It was the first time he had seemed to notice the bird's existence, but he was carrying out a long-formed theory of action with the precision of mature deliberation. The bullfinch, who had fancied himself something of a despot, depressed himself of a sudden into a third of his normal displacement; then he fell to a helpless wing-beating and shrill cheeping. He had cost twenty-seven shillings without the cage, but Lady Anne made no sign of interfering. She had been dead for two hours.

THE LOST SANJAK

THE prison Chaplain entered the condemned's cell for the last time, to give such consolation as he might.

"The only consolation I crave for," said the condemned, "is to tell my story in its entirety to some one who will at least give it a respectful hearing."

"We must not be too long over it," said the Chaplain, looking at his watch.

The condemned repressed a shiver and commenced.

"Most people will be of opinion that I am paying the penalty of my own violent deeds. In reality I am a victim to a lack of specialisation in my education and character."

"Lack of specialisation!" said the Chaplain.

"Yes. If I had been known as one of the few men in England familiar with the fauna of the Outer Hebrides, or able to repeat

stanzas of Camoens' poetry in the original,
I should have had no difficulty in proving
my identity in the crisis when my identity
became a matter of life and death for me.
But my education was merely a moderately
good one, and my temperament was of the
general order that avoids specialisation. I
know a little in a general way about garden-
ing and history and old masters, but I could
never tell you off-hand whether 'Stella van
der Loopen' was a chrysanthemum or a
heroine of the American War of Independence, or something by Romney in the
Louvre."

The Chaplain shifted uneasily in his seat.
Now that the alternatives had been suggested
they all seemed dreadfully possible.

"I fell in love, or thought I did, with the
local doctor's wife," continued the condemned.
"Why I should have done so, I cannot say,
for I do not remember that she possessed
any particular attractions of mind or body.
On looking back at past events it seems to
me that she must have been distinctly
ordinary, but I suppose the doctor had fallen
in love with her once, and what man has
done man can do. She appeared to be
pleased with the attentions which I paid her,

and to that extent I suppose I might say she encouraged me, but I think she was honestly unaware that I meant anything more than a little neighbourly interest. When one is face to face with Death one wishes to be just."

The Chaplain murmured approval. "At any rate, she was genuinely horrified when I took advantage of the doctor's absence one evening to declare what I believed to be my passion. She begged me to pass out of her life, and I could scarcely do otherwise than agree, though I hadn't the dimmest idea of how it was to be done. In novels and plays I knew it was a regular occurrence, and if you mistook a lady's sentiments or intentions you went off to India and did things on the frontier as a matter of course. As I stumbled along the doctor's carriage-drive I had no very clear idea as to what my line of action was to be, but I had a vague feeling that I must look at the *Times* Atlas before going to bed. Then, on the dark and lonely highway, I came suddenly on a dead body."

The Chaplain's interest in the story visibly quickened.

" Judging by the clothes it wore, the corpse

was that of a Salvation Army captain. Some shocking accident seemed to have struck him down, and the head was crushed and battered out of all human semblance. Probably, I thought, a motor-car fatality; and then, with a sudden overmastering insistence, came another thought, that here was a remarkable opportunity for losing my identity and passing out of the life of the doctor's wife for ever. No tiresome and risky voyage to distant lands, but a mere exchange of clothes and identity with the unknown victim of an unwitnessed accident. With considerable difficulty I undressed the corpse, and clothed it anew in my own garments. Any one who has valeted a dead Salvation Army captain in an uncertain light will appreciate the difficulty. With the idea, presumably, of inducing the doctor's wife to leave her husband's roof-tree for some habitation which would be run at my expense, I had crammed my pockets with a store of banknotes, which represented a good deal of my immediate worldly wealth. When, therefore, I stole away into the world in the guise of a nameless Salvationist, I was not without resources which would easily support so humble a rôle for a considerable period. I tramped to a

neighbouring market-town, and, late as the
hour was, the production of a few shillings
procured me supper and a night's lodging
in a cheap coffee-house. The next day I
started forth on an aimless course of wandering from one small town to another. I was
already somewhat disgusted with the upshot
of my sudden freak; in a few hours' time I
was considerably more so. In the contents-
bill of a local news sheet I read the announce-
ment of my own murder at the hands of
some person unknown; on buying a copy
of the paper for a detailed account of the
tragedy, which at first had aroused in me a
certain grim amusement, I found that the
deed was ascribed to a wandering Salvationist
of doubtful antecedents, who had been seen
lurking in the roadway near the scene of the
crime. I was no longer amused. The
matter promised to be embarrassing. What
I had mistaken for a motor accident was
evidently a case of savage assault and
murder, and, until the real culprit was found,
I should have much difficulty in explaining
my intrusion into the affair. Of course I
could establish my own identity; but how,
without disagreeably involving the doctor's
wife, could I give any adequate reason for

2

changing clothes with the murdered man? While my brain worked feverishly at this problem, I subconsciously obeyed a secondary instinct—to get as far away as possible from the scene of the crime, and to get rid at all costs of my incriminating uniform. There I found a difficulty. I tried two or three obscure clothes shops, but my entrance invariably aroused an attitude of hostile suspicion in the proprietors, and on one excuse or another they avoided serving me with the now ardently desired change of clothing. The uniform that I had so thoughtlessly donned seemed as difficult to get out of as the fatal shirt of—— You know, I forget the creature's name."

"Yes, yes," said the Chaplain hurriedly. "Go on with your story."

"Somehow, until I could get out of those compromising garments, I felt it would not be safe to surrender myself to the police. The thing that puzzled me was why no attempt was made to arrest me, since there was no question as to the suspicion which followed me, like an inseparable shadow, wherever I went. Stares, nudgings, whisperings, and even loud-spoken remarks of 'that's 'im' greeted my every appearance, and the

meanest and most deserted eating-house that
I patronised soon became filled with a crowd
of furtively watching customers. I began
to sympathise with the feelings of Royal
personages trying to do a little private
shopping under the unsparing scrutiny of
an irrepressible public. And still, with all
this inarticulate shadowing, which weighed
on my nerves almost worse than open
hostility would have done, no attempt was
made to interfere with my liberty. Later
on I discovered the reason. At the time
of the murder on the lonely highway a series
of important bloodhound trials had been
taking place in the near neighbourhood, and
some dozen and a half couples of trained
animals had been put on the track of the
supposed murderer—on my track. One of
our most public-spirited London dailies had
offered a princely prize to the owner of the pair
that should first track me down, and betting
on the chances of the respective competitors
became rife throughout the land. The dogs
ranged far and wide over about thirteen
counties, and though my own movements
had become by this time perfectly well-known
to police and public alike, the sporting instincts of the nation stepped in to prevent

my premature arrest. " Give the dogs a
chance," was the prevailing sentiment, when-
ever some ambitious local constable wished
to put an end to my drawn-out evasion of
justice. My final capture by the winning
pair was not a very dramatic episode, in
fact, I'm not sure that they would have taken
any notice of me if I hadn't spoken to them
and patted them, but the event gave rise to
an extraordinary amount of partisan excite-
ment. The owner of the pair who were next
nearest up at the finish was an American,
and he lodged a protest on the ground that
an otterhound had married into the family
of the winning pair six generations ago, and
that the prize had been offered to the first
pair of bloodhounds to capture the murderer,
and that a dog that had $\frac{1}{64}$th part of
otterhound blood in it couldn't technically
be considered a bloodhound. I forget how
the matter was ultimately settled, but it
aroused a tremendous amount of acrimonious
discussion on both sides of the Atlantic. My
own contribution to the controversy con-
sisted in pointing out that the whole dispute
was beside the mark, as the actual murderer
had not yet been captured ; but I soon discovered that on this point there was not the

least divergence of public or expert opinion. I had looked forward apprehensively to the proving of my identity and the establishment of my motives as a disagreeable necessity; I speedily found out that the most disagreeable part of the business was that it couldn't be done. When I saw in the glass the haggard and hunted expression which the experiences of the past few weeks had stamped on my erstwhile placid countenance, I could scarcely feel surprised that the few friends and relations I possessed refused to recognise me in my altered guise, and persisted in their obstinate but widely shared belief that it was I who had been done to death on the highway. To make matters worse, infinitely worse, an aunt of the really murdered man, an appalling female of an obviously low order of intelligence, identified me as her nephew, and gave the authorities a lurid account of my depraved youth and of her laudable but unavailing efforts to spank me into a better way. I believe it was even proposed to search me for fingerprints."

"But," said the Chaplain, "surely your educational attainments——"

"That was just the crucial point," said the

condemned; "that was where my lack of specialisation told so fatally against me. The dead Salvationist, whose identity I had so lightly and so disastrously adopted, had possessed a veneer of cheap modern education. It should have been easy to demonstrate that my learning was on altogether another plane to his, but in my nervousness I bungled miserably over test after test that was put to me. The little French I had ever known deserted me; I could not render a simple phrase about the gooseberry of the gardener into that language, because I had forgotten the French for gooseberry."

The Chaplain again wriggled uneasily in his seat. "And then," resumed the condemned, "came the final discomfiture. In our village we had a modest little debating club, and I remembered having promised, chiefly, I suppose, to please and impress the doctor's wife, to give a sketchy kind of lecture on the Balkan Crisis. I had relied on being able to get up my facts from one or two standard works, and the back-numbers of certain periodicals. The prosecution had made a careful note of the circumstance that the man whom I claimed to be—and

actually was — had posed locally as some
sort of second - hand authority on Balkan
affairs, and, in the midst of a string of
questions on indifferent topics, the examining
counsel asked me with a diabolical sudden-
ness if I could tell the Court the whereabouts
of Novibazar. I felt the question to be a
crucial one; something told me that the
answer was St. Petersburg or Baker Street.
I hesitated, looked helplessly round at the
sea of tensely expectant faces, pulled myself
together, and chose Baker Street. And then
I knew that everything was lost. The
prosecution had no difficulty in demon-
strating that an individual, even moderately
versed in the affairs of the Near East, could
never have so unceremoniously dislocated
Novibazar from its accustomed corner of the
map. It was an answer which the Salvation
Army captain might conceivably have made
—and I had made it. The circumstantial
evidence connecting the Salvationist with
the crime was overwhelmingly convincing,
and I had inextricably identified myself with
the Salvationist. And thus it comes to pass
that in ten minutes' time I shall be hanged
by the neck until I am dead in expiation of
the murder of myself, which murder never

took place, and of which, in any case, I am necessarily innocent."

.   .   .   .   .   .

When the Chaplain returned to his quarters some fifteen minutes later, the black flag was floating over the prison tower. Breakfast was waiting for him in the dining-room, but he first passed into his library, and, taking up the *Times* Atlas, consulted a map of the Balkan Peninsula. "A thing like that," he observed, closing the volume with a snap, "might happen to any one."

THE SEX THAT DOESN'T
SHOP

THE opening of a large new centre for West End shopping, particularly feminine shopping, suggests the reflection, Do women ever really shop? Of course, it is a well-attested fact that they go forth shopping as assiduously as a bee goes flower-visiting, but do they shop in the practical sense of the word? Granted the money, time, and energy, a resolute course of shopping transactions would naturally result in having one's ordinary domestic needs unfailingly supplied, whereas it is notorious that women servants (and house-wives of all classes) make it almost a point of honour not to be supplied with everyday necessities. "We shall be out of starch by Thursday," they say with fatalistic fore-boding, and by Thursday they are out of starch. They have predicted almost to a minute the moment when their supply would give out and if Thursday happens to be early closing day their triumph is complete. A shop where starch is stored for retail purposes possibly stands at their very door, but the feminine mind has rejected such an obvious source for replenishing a dwindling stock. "We don't deal there" places it at once beyond the pale of human resort. And it is noteworthy that, just as a sheep-worrying dog seldom molests the flocks in his near neighbourhood, so a woman rarely deals with shops in her immediate vicinity. The more remote the source of supply the more fixed seems to be the resolve to run short of the commodity. The Ark had probably not quitted its last moorings five minutes before some feminine voice gloatingly recorded a shortage of bird-seed. A few days ago two lady acquaintances of mine were confessing to some mental uneasiness because a friend had called just before lunch-time, and they had been unable to ask her to stop and share their meal, as (with a touch of legitimate pride) "there was nothing in the house." I pointed out that they lived in a street that bristled with provision shops and that it would have been easy to mobilise a very passable luncheon in less than five minutes. " That," they said with quiet dignity, "would not have occurred to us," and I felt that I had suggested something bordering on the indecent.

But it is in catering for her literary wants that a woman's shopping capacity breaks down most completely. If you have perchance produced a book which has met with some little measure of success, you are certain to get a letter from some lady whom you scarcely know to bow to, asking you "how it can be got." She knows the name of the book, its author, and who published it, but how to get into actual contact with it is still an unsolved problem to her. You write back pointing out that to have recourse to an ironmonger or a corn-dealer will only entail delay and disappointment, and suggest an application to a bookseller as the most hopeful thing you can think of. In a day or two she writes again: "It is all right; I have borrowed it from your aunt." Here, of course, we have an example of the Beyond-Shopper, one who has learned the Better Way, but the helplessness exists even when such bypaths of relief are closed. A lady who lives in the West End was ex-

pressing to me the other day her interest
in West Highland terriers, and her desire
to know more about the breed, so when, a
few days later, I came across an exhaustive
article on that subject in the current number
of one of our best known outdoor - life
weeklies, I mentioned the circumstance in
a letter, giving the date of that number. " I
cannot get the paper," was her telephoned
response. And she couldn't. She lived in
a city where newsagents are numbered, I
suppose, by the thousand, and she must
have passed dozens of such shops in her
daily shopping excursions, but as far as she
was concerned that article on West Highland
terriers might as well have been written in
a missal stored away in some Buddhist
monastery in Eastern Thibet.

The brutal directness of the masculine
shopper arouses a certain combative derision
in the feminine onlooker. A cat that spreads
one shrew-mouse over the greater part of a
long summer afternoon, and then possibly
loses him, doubtless feels the same contempt
for the terrier who compresses his rat into
ten seconds of the strenuous life. I was
finishing off a short list of purchases a few
afternoons ago when I was discovered by a

lady of my acquaintance whom, swerving aside from the lead given us by her god-parents thirty years ago, we will call Agatha.

"You're surely not buying blotting-paper *here*?" she exclaimed in an agitated whisper, and she seemed so genuinely concerned that I stayed my hand.

"Let me take you to Winks and Pinks," she said as soon as we were out of the building: "they've got such lovely shades of blotting-paper—pearl and heliotrope and *momie* and crushed——"

"But I want ordinary white blotting-paper," I said.

"Never mind. They know me at Winks and Pinks," she replied inconsequently. Agatha apparently has an idea that blotting-paper is only sold in small quantities to persons of known reputation, who may be trusted not to put it to dangerous or improper uses. After walking some two hundred yards she began to feel that her tea was of more immediate importance than my blotting-paper.

"What do you want blotting-paper for?" she asked suddenly. I explained patiently.

"I use it to dry up the ink of wet manuscript without smudging the writing.

Probably a Chinese invention of the second century before Christ, but I'm not sure. The only other use for it that I can think of is to roll it into a ball for a kitten to play with."

"But you haven't got a kitten," said Agatha, with a feminine desire for stating the entire truth on most occasions.

"A stray one might come in at any moment," I replied.

Anyway, I didn't get the blotting-paper.

THE BLOOD-FEUD OF
TOAD-WATER

A WEST-COUNTRY EPIC

THE Cricks lived at Toad-Water; and in
the same lonely upland spot Fate had
pitched the home of the Saunderses, and for
miles around these two dwellings there was
never a neighbour or a chimney or even a
burying-ground to bring a sense of cheerful
communion or social intercourse. Nothing
but fields and spinneys and barns, lanes and
waste-lands. Such was Toad-Water; and,
even so, Toad-Water had its history.

Thrust away in the benighted hinterland
of a scattered market district, it might have
been supposed that these two detached items
of the Great Human Family would have
leaned towards one another in a fellowship
begotten of kindred circumstances and a
common isolation from the outer world.

And perhaps it had been so once, but the way of things had brought it otherwise. Indeed, otherwise. Fate, which had linked the two families in such unavoidable association of habitat, had ordained that the Crick household should nourish and maintain among its earthly possessions sundry head of domestic fowls, while to the Saunderses was given a disposition towards the cultivation of garden crops. Herein lay the material, ready to hand, for the coming of feud and ill-blood. For the grudge between the man of herbs and the man of live stock is no new thing; you will find traces of it in the fourth chapter of Genesis. And one sunny afternoon in late spring-time the feud came—came, as such things mostly do come, with seeming aimlessness and triviality. One of the Crick hens, in obedience to the nomadic instincts of her kind, wearied of her legitimate scratching-grounds, and flew over the low wall that divided the holdings of the neighbours. And there, on the yonder side, with a hurried consciousness that her time and opportunities might be limited, the misguided bird scratched and scraped and beaked and delved in the soft yielding bed that had been prepared for the solace and well-being of a colony of seed-

ling onions. Little showers of earth-mould
and root-fibres went spraying before the hen
and behind her, and every minute the area of
her operations widened. The onions suffered
considerably. Mrs. Saunders, sauntering at
this luckless moment down the garden path,
in order to fill her soul with reproaches at
the iniquity of the weeds, which grew faster
than she or her good man cared to remove
them, stopped in mute discomfiture before
the presence of a more magnificent grievance.
And then, in the hour of her calamity, she
turned instinctively to the Great Mother, and
gathered in her capacious hands large clods
of the hard brown soil that lay at her feet.
With a terrible sincerity of purpose, though
with a contemptible inadequacy of aim, she
rained her earth bolts at the marauder, and
the bursting pellets called forth a flood of
cackling protest and panic from the hastily
departing fowl. Calmness under misfortune
is not an attribute of either hen-folk or
womenkind, and while Mrs. Saunders de-
claimed over her onion bed such portions of
the slang dictionary as are permitted by the
Nonconformist conscience to be said or sung,
the Vasco da Gama fowl was waking the
echoes of Toad-Water with crescendo bursts

3

of throat music which compelled attention to her griefs. Mrs. Crick had a long family, and was therefore licensed, in the eyes of her world, to have a short temper, and when some of her ubiquitous offspring had informed her, with the authority of eye-witnesses, that her neighbour had so far forgotten herself as to heave stones at her hen—her best hen, the best layer in the countryside—her thoughts clothed themselves in language " unbecoming to a Christian woman "—so at least said Mrs. Saunders, to whom most of the language was applied. Nor was she, on her part, surprised at Mrs. Crick's conduct in letting her hens stray into other body's gardens, and then abusing of them, seeing as how she remembered things against Mrs. Crick—and the latter simultaneously had recollections of lurking episodes in the past of Susan Saunders that were nothing to her credit. " Fond memory, when all things fade we fly to thee," and in the paling light of an April afternoon the two women confronted each other from their respective sides of the party wall, recalling with shuddering breath the blots and blemishes of their neighbour's family record. There was that aunt of Mrs. Crick's who had died a pauper in Exeter workhouse—every one knew that Mrs. Saunders' uncle on her mother's side drank himself to death—then there was that Bristol cousin of Mrs. Crick's! From the shrill triumph with which his name was dragged in, his crime must have been pilfering from a cathedral at least, but as both remembrancers were speaking at once it was difficult to distinguish his infamy from the scandal which beclouded the memory of Mrs. Saunders' brother's wife's mother—who may have been a regicide, and was certainly not a nice person as Mrs. Crick painted her. And then, with an air of accumulating and irresistible conviction, each belligerent informed the other that she was no lady—after which they withdrew in a great silence, feeling that nothing further remained to be said. The chaffinches clinked in the apple trees and the bees droned round the berberis bushes, and the waning sunlight slanted pleasantly across the garden plots, but between the neighbour households had sprung up a barrier of hate, permeating and permanent.

The male heads of the families were necessarily drawn into the quarrel, and the children on either side were forbidden to have anything to do with the unhallowed

offspring of the other party. As they had to
travel a good three miles along the same
road to school every day, this was awkward,
but such things have to be. Thus all communication between the households was
sundered. Except the cats. Much as Mrs.
Saunders might deplore it, rumour persist-
ently pointed to the Crick he-cat as the
presumable father of sundry kittens of which
the Saunders she-cat was indisputably the
mother. Mrs. Saunders drowned the kittens,
but the disgrace remained.

Summer succeeded spring, and winter
summer, but the feud outlasted the waning
seasons. Once, indeed, it seemed as though
the healing influences of religion might
restore to Toad-Water its erstwhile peace ;
the hostile families found themselves side by
side in the soul-kindling atmosphere of a
Revival Tea, where hymns were blended
with a beverage that came of tea-leaves and
hot water and took after the latter parent,
and where ghostly counsel was tempered by
garnishings of solidly fashioned buns—and
here, wrought up by the environment of
festive piety, Mrs. Saunders so far unbent as
to remark guardedly to Mrs. Crick that the
evening had been a fine one. Mrs. Crick,

under the influence of her ninth cup of tea
and her fourth hymn, ventured on the hope
that it might continue fine, but a maladroit
allusion on the part of the Saunders good
man to the backwardness of garden crops
brought the Feud stalking forth from its
corner with all its old bitterness. Mrs.
Saunders joined heartily in the singing of the
final hymn, which told of peace and joy
and archangels and golden glories; but her
thoughts were dwelling on the pauper aunt
of Exeter.

Years have rolled away, and some of the
actors in this wayside drama have passed
into the Unknown; other onions have arisen,
have flourished, have gone their way, and the
offending hen has long since expiated her
misdeeds and lain with trussed feet and a
look of ineffable peace under the arched roof
of Barnstaple market.

But the Blood-feud of Toad-Water survives
to this day.

A YOUNG TURKISH
CATASTROPHE

IN TWO SCENES

THE Minister for Fine Arts (to whose Department had been lately added the new sub-section of Electoral Engineering) paid a business visit to the Grand Vizier. According to Eastern etiquette they discoursed for a while on indifferent subjects. The Minister only checked himself in time from making a passing reference to the Marathon Race, remembering that the Vizier had a Persian grandmother and might consider any allusion to Marathon as somewhat tactless. Presently the Minister broached the subject of his interview.

"Under the new Constitution are women to have votes?" he asked suddenly.

"To have votes? Women?" exclaimed the Vizier in some astonishment. "My dear

Pasha, the New Departure has a flavour of the absurd as it is; don't let's try and make it altogether ridiculous. Women have no souls and no intelligence; why on earth should they have votes?"

"I know it sounds absurd," said the Minister, "but they are seriously considering the idea in the West."

"Then they must have a larger equipment of seriousness than I gave them credit for. After a lifetime of specialised effort in maintaining my gravity I can scarcely restrain an inclination to smile at the suggestion. Why, our womenfolk in most cases don't know how to read or write. How could they perform the operation of voting?"

"They could be shown the names of the candidates and where to make their cross."

"I beg your pardon?" interrupted the Vizier.

"Their crescent, I mean," corrected the Minister. "It would be to the liking of the Young Turkish Party," he added.

"Oh, well," said the Vizier, "if we are to do the thing at all we may as well go the whole h——" he pulled up just as he was uttering the name of an unclean animal, and continued, "the complete camel. I will issue instructions that womenfolk are to have votes."

.   .   .   .   .   .

The poll was drawing to a close in the Lakoumistan division. The candidate of the Young Turkish Party was known to be three or four hundred votes ahead, and he was already drafting his address, returning thanks to the electors. His victory had been almost a foregone conclusion, for he had set in motion all the approved electioneering machinery of the West. He had even employed motor-cars. Few of his supporters had gone to the poll in these vehicles, but, thanks to the intelligent driving of his chauffeurs, many of his opponents had gone to their graves or to the local hospitals, or otherwise abstained from voting. And then something unlooked-for happened. The rival candidate, Ali the Blest, arrived on the scene with his wives and womenfolk, who numbered, roughly, six hundred. Ali had wasted little effort on election literature, but had been heard to remark that every vote given to his opponent meant another sack thrown into the Bosphorus. The Young Turkish candidate, who had conformed to the Western custom of one wife and hardly any mistresses, stood by helplessly while his adversary's poll swelled to a triumphant majority.

"Cristabel Columbus!" he exclaimed, invoking in some confusion the name of a distinguished pioneer; "who would have thought it?"

"Strange," mused Ali, "that one who harangued so clamorously about the Secret Ballot should have overlooked the Veiled Vote."

And, walking homeward with his constituents, he murmured in his beard an improvisation on the heretic poet of Persia:

"One, rich in metaphors, his Cause contrives
To urge with edgèd words, like Kabul knives;
And I, who worst him in this sorry game,
Was never rich in anything but—wives."

JUDKIN OF THE PARCELS

A FIGURE in an indefinite tweed suit, carrying brown-paper parcels. That is what we met suddenly, at the bend of a muddy Dorsetshire lane, and the roan mare stared and obviously thought of a curtsey. The mare is road-shy, with intervals of stolidity, and there is no telling what she will pass and what she won't. We call her Redford. That was my first meeting with Judkin, and the next time the circumstances were the same; the same muddy lane, the same rather apologetic figure in the tweed suit, the same—or very similar—parcels. Only this time the roan looked straight in front of her.

Whether I asked the groom or whether he advanced the information, I forget; but someway I gradually reconstructed the life-history of this trudger of the lanes. It was much the same, no doubt, as that of many

others who are from time to time pointed out
to one as having been aforetime in crack
cavalry regiments and noted performers in the
saddle ; men who have breathed into their
lungs the wonder of the East, have romped
through life as through a cotillon, have had
a thrust perhaps at the Viceroy's Cup, and
done fantastic horsefleshy things around the
Gulf of Aden. And then a golden stream
has dried up, the sunlight has faded suddenly
out of things, and the gods have nodded
" Go." And they have not gone. They
have turned instead to the muddy lanes and
cheap villas and the marked-down ills of life,
to watch pear trees growing and to encourage
hens for their eggs. And Judkin was even
as these others ; the wine had been suddenly
spilt from his cup of life, and he had stayed
to suck at the dregs which the wise throw
away. In the days of his scorn for most
things he would have stared the roan mare
and her turn-out out of all pretension to
smartness, as he would have frozen a cheap
claret behind its cork, or a plain woman
behind her veil ; and now he was walking
stoically through the mud, in a tweed suit
that would eventually go on to the gardener's
boy, and would perhaps fit him. The dear

gods, who know the end before the beginning, were perhaps growing a gardener's boy somewhere to fit the garments, and Judkin was only a caretaker, inhabiting a portion of them. That is what I like to think, and I am probably wrong. And Judkin, whose clothes had been to him once more than a religion, scarcely less sacred than a family quarrel, would carry those parcels back to his villa and to the wife who awaited him and them—a wife who may, for all we know to the contrary, have had a figure once, and perhaps has yet a heart of gold—of nine-carat gold, let us say at the least—but assuredly a soul of tape. And he that has fetched and carried will explain how it has fared with him in his dealings, and if he has brought the wrong sort of sugar or thread he will wheedle away the displeasure from that leaden face as a pastrycook girl will drive bluebottles off a stale bun. And that man has known what it was to coax the fret of a thoroughbred, to soothe its toss and sweat as it danced beneath him in the glee and chafe of its pulses and the glory of its thews. He has been in the raw places of the earth, where the desert beasts have whimpered their unthinkable psalmody, and their eyes

have shone back the reflex of the midnight
stars—and he can immerse himself in the
tending of an incubator. It is horrible and
wrong, and yet when I have met him in the
lanes his face has worn a look of tedious
cheerfulness that might pass for happiness.
Has Judkin of the Parcels found something
in the lees of life that I have missed in going
to and fro over many waters? Is there
more wisdom in his perverseness than in the
madness of the wise? The dear gods know.

I don't think I saw Judkin more than three
times all told, and always the lane was our
point of contact; but as the roan mare was
taking me to the station one heavy, cloud-
smeared day, I passed a dull-looking villa
that the groom, or instinct, told me was
Judkin's home. From beyond a hedge of
ragged elder-bushes could be heard the thud,
thud of a spade, with an occasional clink and
pause, as if some one had picked out a stone
and thrown it to a distance, and I knew that
he was doing nameless things to the roots of
a pear tree. Near by him, I felt sure, would
be lying a large and late vegetable marrow,
and its largeness and lateness would be a
theme of conversation at luncheon. It would
be suggested that it should grace the harvest

thanksgiving service ; the harvest having been so generally unsatisfactory, it would be unfair to let the farmers supply all the material for rejoicing.

And while I was speeding townwards along the rails Judkin would be plodding his way to the vicarage bearing a vegetable marrow and a basketful of dahlias. The basket to be returned.

GABRIEL-ERNEST

"THERE is a wild beast in your woods," said the artist Cunningham, as he was being driven to the station. It was the only remark he had made during the drive, but as Van Cheele had talked incessantly his companion's silence had not been noticeable.

"A stray fox or two and some resident weasels. Nothing more formidable," said Van Cheele. The artist said nothing.

"What did you mean about a wild beast?" said Van Cheele later, when they were on the platform.

"Nothing. My imagination. Here is the train," said Cunningham.

That afternoon Van Cheele went for one of his frequent rambles through his woodland property. He had a stuffed bittern in his study, and knew the names of quite a number of wild flowers, so his aunt had

possibly some justification in describing him
as a great naturalist. At any rate, he was
a great walker. It was his custom to take
mental notes of everything he saw during his
walks, not so much for the purpose of assist-
ing contemporary science as to provide topics
for conversation afterwards. When the blue-
bells began to show themselves in flower he
made a point of informing every one of the
fact; the season of the year might have warned
his hearers of the likelihood of such an occurrence, but at least they felt that he was being
absolutely frank with them.

What Van Cheele saw on this particular
afternoon was, however, something far removed from his ordinary range of experience.
On a shelf of smooth stone overhanging a
deep pool in the hollow of an oak coppice a
boy of about sixteen lay asprawl, drying his
wet brown limbs luxuriously in the sun. His
wet hair, parted by a recent dive, lay close
to his head, and his light-brown eyes, so light
that there was an almost tigerish gleam in
them, were turned towards Van Cheele with a
certain lazy watchfulness. It was an unex-
pected apparition, and Van Cheele found
himself engaged in the novel process of
thinking before he spoke. Where on earth

could this wild-looking boy hail from? The miller's wife had lost a child some two months ago, supposed to have been swept away by the mill-race, but that had been a mere baby, not a half-grown lad.

"What are you doing there?" he demanded.

"Obviously, sunning myself," replied the boy.

"Where do you live?"

"Here, in these woods."

"You can't live in the woods," said Van Cheele.

"They are very nice woods," said the boy, with a touch of patronage in his voice.

"But where do you sleep at night?"

"I don't sleep at night; that's my busiest time."

Van Cheele began to have an irritated feeling that he was grappling with a problem that was eluding him.

"What do you feed on?" he asked.

"Flesh," said the boy, and he pronounced the word with slow relish, as though he were tasting it.

"Flesh! What flesh?"

"Since it interests you, rabbits, wild-fowl, hares, poultry, lambs in their season, children

4

when I can get any; they're usually too well locked in at night, when I do most of my hunting. It's quite two months since I tasted child-flesh."

Ignoring the chaffing nature of the last remark Van Cheele tried to draw the boy on the subject of possible poaching operations.

"You're talking rather through your hat when you speak of feeding on hares." (Considering the nature of the boy's toilet the simile was hardly an apt one.) "Our hillside hares aren't easily caught."

"At night I hunt on four feet," was the somewhat cryptic response.

"I suppose you mean that you hunt with a dog?" hazarded Van Cheele.

The boy rolled slowly over on to his back, and laughed a weird low laugh, that was pleasantly like a chuckle and disagreeably like a snarl.

"I don't fancy any dog would be very anxious for my company, especially at night."

Van Cheele began to feel that there was something positively uncanny about the strange-eyed, strange-tongued youngster.

"I can't have you staying in these woods," he declared authoritatively.

"I fancy you'd rather have me here than in your house," said the boy.

The prospect of this wild, nude animal in Van Cheele's primly ordered house was certainly an alarming one.

"If you don't go I shall have to make you," said Van Cheele.

The boy turned like a flash, plunged into the pool, and in a moment had flung his wet and glistening body half-way up the bank where Van Cheele was standing. In an otter the movement would not have been remarkable; in a boy Van Cheele found it sufficiently startling. His foot slipped as he made an involuntarily backward movement, and he found himself almost prostrate on the slippery weed-grown bank, with those tigerish yellow eyes not very far from his own. Almost instinctively he half raised his hand to his throat. The boy laughed again, a laugh in which the snarl had nearly driven out the chuckle, and then, with another of his astonishing lightning movements, plunged out of view into a yielding tangle of weed and fern.

"What an extraordinary wild animal!" said Van Cheele as he picked himself up. And then he recalled Cunningham's remark "There is a wild beast in your woods."

Walking slowly homeward, Van Cheele
began to turn over in his mind various local
occurrences which might be traceable to the
existence of this astonishing young savage.

Something had been thinning the game in
the woods lately, poultry had been missing
from the farms, hares were growing unaccount-
ably scarcer, and complaints had reached him
of lambs being carried off bodily from the
hills.   Was it possible that this wild boy was
really hunting the countryside in company
with some clever poacher dog? He had
spoken of hunting " four-footed " by night, but
then, again, he had hinted strangely at no
dog caring to come near him, " especially
at night."   It was certainly puzzling.   And
then, as Van Cheele ran his mind over the
various depredations that had been com-
mitted during the last month or two, he came
suddenly to a dead stop, alike in his walk
and his speculations.   The child missing
from the mill two months ago—the accepted
theory was that it had tumbled into the mill-
race and been swept away; but the mother
had always declared she had heard a shriek
on the hill side of the house, in the opposite
direction from the water.   It was unthinkable, of course, but he wished that the boy

had not made that uncanny remark about child-flesh eaten two months ago. Such dreadful things should not be said even in fun.

Van Cheele, contrary to his usual wont, did not feel disposed to be communicative about his discovery in the wood. His position as a parish councillor and justice of the peace seemed somehow compromised by the fact that he was harbouring a personality of such doubtful repute on his property; there was even a possibility that a heavy bill of damages for raided lambs and poultry might be laid at his door. At dinner that night he was quite unusually silent.

"Where's your voice gone to?" said his aunt. "One would think you had seen a wolf."

Van Cheele, who was not familiar with the old saying, thought the remark rather foolish; if he *had* seen a wolf on his property his tongue would have been extraordinarily busy with the subject.

At breakfast next morning Van Cheele was conscious that his feeling of uneasiness regarding yesterday's episode had not wholly disappeared, and he resolved to go by train to the neighbouring cathedral town, hunt up

Cunningham, and learn from him what he had really seen that had prompted the remark about a wild beast in the woods. With this resolution taken, his usual cheerfulness partially returned, and he hummed a bright little melody as he sauntered to the morning-room for his customary cigarette. As he entered the room the melody made way abruptly for a pious invocation. Gracefully asprawl on the ottoman, in an attitude of almost exaggerated repose, was the boy of the woods. He was drier than when Van Cheele had last seen him, but no other alteration was noticeable in his toilet.

" How dare you come here ? " asked Van Cheele furiously.

" You told me I was not to stay in the woods," said the boy calmly.

" But not to come here. Supposing my aunt should see you ! "

And with a view to minimising that catastrophe, Van Cheele hastily obscured as much of his unwelcome guest as possible under the folds of a *Morning Post*. At that moment his aunt entered the room.

" This is a poor boy who has lost his way— and lost his memory. He doesn't know who he is or where he comes from," explained Van

Cheele desperately, glancing apprehensively at the waif's face to see whether he was going to add inconvenient candour to his other savage propensities.

Miss Van Cheele was enormously interested.

"Perhaps his underlinen is marked," she suggested.

"He seems to have lost most of that, too," said Van Cheele, making frantic little grabs at the *Morning Post* to keep it in its place.

A naked homeless child appealed to Miss Van Cheele as warmly as a stray kitten or derelict puppy would have done.

"We must do all we can for him," she decided, and in a very short time a messenger, dispatched to the rectory, where a page-boy was kept, had returned with a suit of pantry clothes, and the necessary accessories of shirt, shoes, collar, etc. Clothed, clean, and groomed, the boy lost none of his uncanniness in Van Cheele's eyes, but his aunt found him sweet.

"We must call him something till we know who he really is," she said. "Gabriel-Ernest, I think ; those are nice suitable names."

Van Cheele agreed, but he privately doubted whether they were being grafted on to a nice suitable child. His misgivings were not diminished by the fact that his staid and elderly spaniel had bolted out of the house at the first incoming of the boy, and now obstinately remained shivering and yapping at the farther end of the orchard, while the canary, usually as vocally industrious as Van Cheele himself, had put itself on an allowance of frightened cheeps. More than ever he was resolved to consult Cunningham without loss of time.

As he drove off to the station his aunt was arranging that Gabriel-Ernest should help her to entertain the infant members of her Sunday-school class at tea that afternoon.

Cunningham was not at first disposed to be communicative.

"My mother died of some brain trouble," he explained, "so you will understand why I am averse to dwelling on anything of an impossibly fantastic nature that I may see or think that I have seen."

"But what *did* you see?" persisted Van Cheele.

"What I thought I saw was something so extraordinary that no really sane man could dignify it with the credit of having actually happened. I was standing, the last evening I was with you, half-hidden in the hedge-growth by the orchard gate, watching the dying glow of the sunset. Suddenly I became aware of a naked boy, a bather from some neighbouring pool, I took him to be, who was standing out on the bare hillside also watching the sunset. His pose was so suggestive of some wild faun of Pagan myth that I instantly wanted to engage him as a model, and in another moment I think I should have hailed him. But just then the sun dipped out of view, and all the orange and pink slid out of the landscape, leaving it cold and grey. And at the same moment an astounding thing happened—the boy vanished too!"

"What! vanished away into nothing?" asked Van Cheele excitedly.

"No; that is the dreadful part of it," answered the artist; "on the open hillside where the boy had been standing a second ago, stood a large wolf, blackish in colour, with gleaming fangs and cruel, yellow eyes. You may think——"

But Van Cheele did not stop for anything as futile as thought. Already he was tearing at top speed towards the station. He dismissed the idea of a telegram. "Gabriel-Ernest is a werewolf" was a hopelessly inadequate effort at conveying the situation, and his aunt would think it was a code message to which he had omitted to give her the key. His one hope was that he might reach home before sundown. The cab which he chartered at the other end of the railway journey bore him with what seemed exasperating slowness along the country roads, which were pink and mauve with the flush of the sinking sun. His aunt was putting away some unfinished jams and cake when he arrived.

"Where is Gabriel-Ernest?" he almost screamed.

"He is taking the little Toop child home," said his aunt. "It was getting so late, I thought it wasn't safe to let it go back alone. What a lovely sunset, isn't it?"

But Van Cheele, although not oblivious of the glow in the western sky, did not stay to discuss its beauties. At a speed for which he was scarcely geared he raced along the narrow lane that led to the home of the Toops. On one side ran the swift current of the mill-stream, on the other rose the stretch of bare hillside. A dwindling rim of red sun showed still on the skyline, and the next turning must bring him in view of the ill-assorted couple he was pursuing. Then the colour went suddenly out of things, and a grey light settled itself with a quick shiver over the landscape. Van Cheele heard a shrill wail of fear, and stopped running.

Nothing was ever seen again of the Toop child or Gabriel-Ernest, but the latter's discarded garments were found lying in the road so it was assumed that the child had fallen into the water, and that the boy had stripped and jumped in, in a vain endeavour to save it. Van Cheele and some workmen who were near by at the time testified to having heard a child scream loudly just near the spot where the clothes were found. Mrs. Toop, who had eleven other children, was decently resigned to her bereavement, but Miss Van Cheele sincerely mourned her lost foundling. It was on her initiative that a memorial brass was put up in the parish church to "Gabriel-Ernest, an unknown boy, who bravely sacrificed his life for another."

Van Cheele gave way to his aunt in most things, but he flatly refused to subscribe to the Gabriel-Ernest memorial.

THE SAINT AND THE
GOBLIN

THE little stone Saint occupied a retired niche in a side aisle of the old cathedral. No one quite remembered who he had been, but that in a way was a guarantee of respectability. At least so the Goblin said. The Goblin was a very fine specimen of quaint stone carving, and lived up in the corbel on the wall opposite the niche of the little Saint. He was connected with some of the best cathedral folk, such as the queer carvings in the choir stalls and chancel screen, and even the gargoyles high up on the roof. All the fantastic beasts and manikins that sprawled and twisted in wood or stone or lead overhead in the arches or away down in the crypt were in some way akin to him; consequently he was a person of recognised importance in the cathedral world.

The little stone Saint and the Goblin got

on very well together, though they looked at most things from different points of view. The Saint was a philanthropist in an old-fashioned way ; he thought the world, as he saw it, was good, but might be improved. In particular he pitied the church mice, who were miserably poor. The Goblin, on the other hand, was of opinion that the world, as he knew it, was bad, but had better be let alone. It was the function of the church mice to be poor.

" All the same," said the Saint, " I feel very sorry for them."

" Of course you do," said the Goblin ; " it's *your* function to feel sorry for them. If they were to leave off being poor you couldn't fulfil your functions. You'd be a sinecure."

He rather hoped that the Saint would ask him what a sinecure meant, but the latter took refuge in a stony silence. The Goblin might be right, but still, he thought, he would like to do something for the church mice before winter came on ; they were so very poor.

Whilst he was thinking the matter over he was startled by something falling between his feet with a hard metallic clatter. It was a bright new thaler; one of the cathedral jackdaws, who collected such things, had flown in with it to a stone cornice just above his niche, and the banging of the sacristy door had startled him into dropping it. Since the invention of gunpowder the family nerves were not what they had been.

"What have you got there?" asked the Goblin.

"A silver thaler," said the Saint. "Really," he continued, "it is most fortunate; now I can do something for the church mice."

"How will you manage it?" asked the Goblin.

The Saint considered.

"I will appear in a vision to the vergeress who sweeps the floors. I will tell her that she will find a silver thaler between my feet, and that she must take it and buy a measure of corn and put it on my shrine. When she finds the money she will know that it was a true dream, and she will take care to follow my directions. Then the mice will have food all the winter."

"Of course *you* can do that," observed the Goblin. "Now, *I* can only appear to people after they have had a heavy supper of indigestible things. My opportunities with the vergeress would be limited. There is some advantage in being a saint after all."

All this while the coin was lying at the Saint's feet. It was clean and glittering and had the Elector's arms beautifully stamped upon it. The Saint began to reflect that such an opportunity was too rare to be hastily disposed of. Perhaps indiscriminate charity might be harmful to the church mice. After all, it was their function to be poor; the Goblin had said so, and the Goblin was generally right.

"I've been thinking," he said to that personage, "that perhaps it would be really better if I ordered a thaler's worth of candles to be placed on my shrine instead of the corn."

He often wished, for the look of the thing, that people would sometimes burn candles at his shrine; but as they had forgotten who he was it was not considered a profitable speculation to pay him that attention.

"Candles would be more orthodox," said the Goblin.

"More orthodox, certainly," agreed the Saint, "and the mice could have the ends to eat; candle-ends are most fattening."

The Goblin was too well bred to wink

besides, being a stone goblin, it was out of the question.

.   .   .   .   .   .

"Well, if it ain't there, sure enough!" said the vergeress next morning. She took the shining coin down from the dusty niche and turned it over and over in her grimy hands. Then she put it to her mouth and bit it.

"She can't be going to eat it," thought the Saint, and fixed her with his stoniest stare.

"Well," said the woman, in a somewhat shriller key, "who'd have thought it! A saint, too!"

Then she did an unaccountable thing. She hunted an old piece of tape out of her pocket, and tied it crosswise, with a big loop, round the thaler, and hung it round the neck of the little Saint.

Then she went away.

"The only possible explanation," said the Goblin, "is that it's a bad one."

.   .   .   .   ,   .

"What is that decoration your neighbour is wearing?" asked a wyvern that was wrought into the capital of an adjacent pillar.

The Saint was ready to cry with mortification, only, being of stone, he couldn't.

"It's a coin of—ahem!—fabulous value," replied the Goblin tactfully.

And the news went round the Cathedral that the shrine of the little stone Saint had been enriched by a priceless offering.

"After all, it's something to have the conscience of a goblin," said the Saint to himself.

The church mice were as poor as ever. But that was their function.

THE SOUL OF LAPLOSHKA

LAPLOSHKA was one of the meanest men I have ever met, and quite one of the most entertaining. He said horrid things about other people in such a charming way that one forgave him for the equally horrid things he said about oneself behind one's back. Hating anything in the way of ill-natured gossip ourselves, we are always grateful to those who do it for us and do it well. And Laploshka did it really well.

Naturally Laploshka had a large circle of acquaintances, and as he exercised some care in their selection it followed that an appreciable proportion were men whose bank balances enabled them to acquiesce indulgently in his rather one-sided views on hospitality. Thus, although possessed of only moderate means, he was able to live comfortably within his income, and still more comfortably within those of various tolerantly disposed associates.

But towards the poor or to those of the same limited resources as himself his attitude was one of watchful anxiety; he seemed to be haunted by a besetting fear lest some fraction of a shilling or franc, or whatever the prevailing coinage might be, should be diverted from his pocket or service into that of a hard-up companion. A two-franc cigar would be cheerfully offered to a wealthy patron, on the principle of doing evil that good may come, but I have known him indulge in agonies of perjury rather than admit the incriminating possession of a copper coin when change was needed to tip a waiter. The coin would have been duly returned at the earliest opportunity—he would have taken means to insure against forgetfulness on the part of the borrower—but accidents might happen, and even the temporary estrangement from his penny or sou was a calamity to be avoided.

The knowledge of this amiable weakness offered a perpetual temptation to play upon Laploshka's fears of involuntary generosity. To offer him a lift in a cab and pretend not to have enough money to pay the fair, to fluster him with a request for a sixpence when his hand was full of silver just received in

change, these were a few of the petty torments
that ingenuity prompted as occasion afforded.
To do justice to Laploshka's resourcefulness
it must be admitted that he always emerged
somehow or other from the most embarrassing
dilemma without in any way compromising
his reputation for saying "No." But the
gods send opportunities at some time to most
men, and mine came one evening when
Laploshka and I were supping together in a
cheap boulevard restaurant. (Except when
he was the bidden guest of some one with an
irreproachable income, Laploshka was wont to
curb his appetite for high living; on such
fortunate occasions he let it go on an easy
snaffle.)   At the conclusion of the meal a
somewhat urgent message called me away,
and without heeding my companion's agitated
protest, I called back cruelly, " Pay my share;
I'll settle with you to-morrow." Early on
the morrow Laploshka hunted me down by
instinct as I walked along a side street that I
hardly ever frequented.   He had the air of a
man who had not slept.

"You owe me two francs from last night,"
was his breathless greeting.

I spoke evasively of the situation in Portugal,
where more trouble seemed brewing.   But

Laploshka listened with the abstraction of the deaf adder, and quickly returned to the subject of the two francs.

"I'm afraid I must owe it to you," I said lightly and brutally. "I haven't a sou in the world," and I added mendaciously, "I'm going away for six months or perhaps longer."

Laploshka said nothing, but his eyes bulged a little and his cheeks took on the mottled hues of an ethnographical map of the Balkan Peninsula. That same day, at sundown, he died. "Failure of the heart's action," was the doctor's verdict; but I, who knew better, knew that he had died of grief.

There arose the problem of what to do with his two francs. To have killed Laploshka was one thing; to have kept his beloved money would have argued a callousness of feeling of which I am not capable. The ordinary solution, of giving it to the poor, would by no means fit the present situation, for nothing would have distressed the dead man more than such a misuse of his property. On the other hand, the bestowal of two francs on the rich was an operation which called for some tact. An easy way out of the difficulty seemed, however, to present itself the following

Sunday, as I was wedged into the cosmopolitan crowd which filled the side-aisle of one of the most popular Paris churches. A collecting-bag, for " the poor of Monsieur le Curé," was buffeting its tortuous way across the seemingly impenetrable human sea, and a German in front of me, who evidently did not wish his appreciation of the magnificent music to be marred by a suggestion of payment, made audible criticisms to his companion on the claims of the said charity.

" They do not want money," he said ; " they have too much money. They have no poor. They are all pampered."

If that were really the case my way seemed clear. I dropped Laploshka's two francs into the bag with a murmured blessing on the rich of Monsieur le Curé.

Some three weeks later chance had taken me to Vienna, and I sat one evening regaling myself in a humble but excellent little Gasthaus up in the Währinger quarter. The appointments were primitive, but the Schnitzel, the beer, and the cheese could not have been improved on. Good cheer brought good custom, and with the exception of one small table near the door every place was occupied. Half-way through my meal I happened to glance in the direction of that empty seat, and saw that it was no longer empty. Poring over the bill of fare with the absorbed scrutiny of one who seeks the cheapest among the cheap was Laploshka. Once he looked across at me, with a comprehensive glance at my repast, as though to say, " It is my two francs you are eating," and then looked swiftly away. Evidently the poor of Monsieur le Curé had been genuine poor. The Schnitzel turned to leather in my mouth, the beer seemed tepid ; I left the Emmenthaler untasted. My one idea was to get away from the room, away from the table where *that* was seated ; and as I fled I felt Laploshka's reproachful eyes watching the amount that I gave to the piccolo—out of his two francs. I lunched next day at an expensive restaurant which I felt sure that the living Laploshka would never have entered on his own account, and I hoped that the dead Laploshka would observe the same barriers. I was not mistaken, but as I came out I found him miserably studying the bill of fare stuck up on the portals. Then he slowly made his way over to a milk-hall. For the first time in my experience I missed the charm and gaiety of Vienna life.

After that, in Paris or London or wherever

I happened to be, I continued to see a good deal of Laploshka. If I had a seat in a box at a theatre I was always conscious of his eyes furtively watching me from the dim recesses of the gallery. As I turned into my club on a rainy afternoon I would see him taking inadequate shelter in a doorway opposite. Even if I indulged in the modest luxury of a penny chair in the Park he generally confronted me from one of the free benches, never staring at me, but always elaborately conscious of my presence. My friends began to comment on my changed looks, and advised me to leave off heaps of things. I should have liked to have left off Laploshka.

On a certain Sunday—it was probably Easter, for the crush was worse than ever—I was again wedged into the crowd listening to the music in the fashionable Paris church, and again the collection-bag was buffeting its way across the human sea. An English lady behind me was making ineffectual efforts to convey a coin into the still distant bag, so I took the money at her request and helped it forward to its destination. It was a two-franc piece. A swift inspiration came to me, and I merely dropped my own sou into the bag and slid the silver coin into my pocket. I had withdrawn Laploshka's two francs from the poor, who should never have had that legacy. As I backed away from the crowd I heard a woman's voice say, "I don't believe he put my money in the bag. There are swarms of people in Paris like that!" But my mind was lighter than it had been for a long time.

The delicate mission of bestowing the retrieved sum on the deserving rich still confronted me. Again I trusted to the inspiration of accident, and again fortune favoured me. A shower drove me, two days later, into one of the historic churches on the left bank of the Seine, and there I found, peering at the old wood-carvings, the Baron R., one of the wealthiest and most shabbily dressed men in Paris. It was now or never. Putting a strong American inflection into the French which I usually talked with an unmistakable British accent, I catechised the Baron as to the date of the church's building, its dimensions, and other details which an American tourist would be certain to want to know. Having acquired such information as the Baron was able to impart on short notice, I solemnly placed the two-franc piece in his hand, with the hearty assurance that it was " pour vous," and turned to go. The Baron was slightly taken aback, but accepted the situation with a good grace. Walking over to a small box fixed in the wall, he dropped Laploshka's two francs into the slot. Over the box was the inscription, " Pour les pauvres de M. le Curé."

That evening, at the crowded corner by the Café de la Paix, I caught a fleeting glimpse of Laploshka. He smiled, slightly raised his hat, and vanished. I never saw him again. After all, the money had been *given* to the deserving rich, and the soul of Laploshka was at peace.

THE BAG

"THE Major is coming in to tea," said Mrs. Hoopington to her niece. "He's just gone round to the stables with his horse. Be as bright and lively as you can; the poor man's got a fit of the glooms."

Major Pallaby was a victim of circumstances, over which he had no control, and of his temper, over which he had very little. He had taken on the Mastership of the Pexdale Hounds in succession to a highly popular man who had fallen foul of his committee, and the Major found himself confronted with the overt hostility of at least half the hunt, while his lack of tact and amiability had done much to alienate the remainder. Hence subscriptions were beginning to fall off, foxes grew provokingly scarcer, and wire obtruded itself with increasing frequency. The Major could plead reasonable excuse for his fit of the glooms.

In ranging herself as a partisan on the side of Major Pallaby Mrs. Hoopington had been largely influenced by the fact that she had made up her mind to marry him at an early date. Against his notorious bad temper she set his three thousand a year, and his prospective succession to a baronetcy gave a casting vote in his favour. The Major's plans on the subject of matrimony were not at present in such an advanced stage as Mrs. Hoopington's, but he was beginning to find his way over to Hoopington Hall with a frequency that was already being commented on.

"He had a wretchedly thin field out again yesterday," said Mrs. Hoopington. "Why you didn't bring one or two hunting men down with you, instead of that stupid Russian boy, I can't think."

"Vladimir isn't stupid," protested her niece; "he's one of the most amusing boys I ever met. Just compare him for a moment with some of your heavy hunting men——"

"Anyhow, my dear Norah, he can't ride."

"Russians never can; but he shoots."

"Yes; and what does he shoot? Yesterday he brought home a woodpecker in his game-bag."

" But he'd shot three pheasants and some rabbits as well."

" That's no excuse for including a woodpecker in his game-bag."

" Foreigners go in for mixed bags more than we do. A Grand Duke pots a vulture just as seriously as we should stalk a bustard. Anyhow, I've explained to Vladimir that certain birds are beneath his dignity as a sportsman. And as he's only nineteen, of course, his dignity is a sure thing to appeal to."

Mrs. Hoopington sniffed. Most people with whom Vladimir came in contact found his high spirits infectious, but his present hostess was guaranteed immune against infection of that sort.

" I hear him coming in now," she observed. " I shall go and get ready for tea. We're going to have it here in the hall. Entertain the Major if he comes in before I'm down, and, above all, be bright."

Norah was dependent on her aunt's good graces for many little things that made life worth living, and she was conscious of a feeling of discomfiture because the Russian youth whom she had brought down as a welcome element of change in the country-house routine was not making a good impression. That young gentleman, however, was supremely unconscious of any shortcomings, and burst into the hall, tired, and less sprucely groomed than usual, but distinctly radiant. His game - bag looked comfortably full.

"Guess what I have shot," he demanded.

"Pheasants, woodpigeons, rabbits," hazarded Norah.

"No; a large beast; I don't know what you call it in English. Brown, with a darkish tail." Norah changed colour.

"Does it live in a tree and eat nuts?" she asked, hoping that the use of the adjective "large" might be an exaggeration.

Vladimir laughed.

"Oh no ; not a *biyelka*."

"Does it swim and eat fish?" asked Norah, with a fervent prayer in her heart that it might turn out to be an otter.

"No," said Vladimir, busy with the straps of his game-bag; "it lives in the woods, and eats rabbits and chickens."

Norah sat down suddenly, and hid her face in her hands.

"Merciful Heaven!" she wailed ; "he's shot a fox!"

Vladimir looked up at her in consternation.
In a torrent of agitated words she tried to
explain the horror of the situation. The boy
understood nothing, but was thoroughly
alarmed.

" Hide it, hide it ! " said Norah frantically,
pointing to the still unopened bag. " My
aunt and the Major will be here in a moment.
Throw it on the top of that chest ; they won't
see it there."

Vladimir swung the bag with fair aim ; but
the strap caught in its flight on the out-
standing point of an antler fixed in the wall,
and the bag, with its terrible burden, remained
suspended just above the alcove where tea
would presently be laid. At that moment
Mrs. Hoopington and the Major entered the
hall.

" The Major is going to draw our covers
to-morrow," announced the lady, with a certain
heavy satisfaction. " Smithers is confident
that we'll be able to show him some sport ;
he swears he's seen a fox in the nut copse
three times this week."

" I'm sure I hope so ; I hope so," said the
Major moodily. " I must break this sequence
of blank days. One hears so often that a fox
has settled down as a tenant for life in certain

covers, and then when you go to turn him
out there isn't a trace of him. I'm certain a
fox was shot or trapped in Lady Widden's
woods the very day before we drew them."

" Major, if any one tried that game on in
my woods they'd get short shrift," said Mrs.
Hoopington.

Norah found her way mechanically to the
tea-table and made her fingers frantically
busy in rearranging the parsley round the
sandwich dish. On one side of her loomed
the morose countenance of the Major, on the
other she was conscious of the scared, miserable eyes of Vladimir. And above it all hung
that. She dared not raise her eyes above the
level of the tea-table, and she almost expected
to see a spot of accusing vulpine blood drip
down and stain the whiteness of the cloth.
Her aunt's manner signalled to her the re-
peated message to " be bright "; for the
present she was fully occupied in keeping her
teeth from chattering.

" What did you shoot to-day ? " asked Mrs.
Hoopington suddenly of the unusually silent
Vladimir.

" Nothing—nothing worth speaking of,"
said the boy.

Norah's heart, which had stood still for a

space, made up for lost time with a most
disturbing bound.

"I wish you'd find something that was
worth speaking about," said the hostess;
"every one seems to have lost their tongues."

"When did Smithers last see that fox?"
said the Major.

"Yesterday morning; a fine dog-fox, with
a dark brush," confided Mrs. Hoopington.

"Aha, we'll have a good gallop after that
brush to-morrow," said the Major, with a
transient gleam of good humour. And then
gloomy silence settled again round the tea-
table, a silence broken only by despondent
munchings and the occasional feverish rattle
of a teaspoon in its saucer. A diversion was
at last afforded by Mrs. Hoopington's fox-
terrier, which had jumped on to a vacant
chair, the better to survey the delicacies of the
table, and was now sniffing in an upward
direction at something apparently more interesting than cold tea-cake.

"What is exciting him?" asked his mistress, as the dog suddenly broke into short
angry barks, with a running accompaniment
of tremulous whines.

"Why," she continued, "it's your game-
bag, Vladimir! What *have* you got in it?"

6

"By Gad," said the Major, who was now standing up; "there's a pretty warm scent!"

And then a simultaneous idea flashed on himself and Mrs. Hoopington. Their faces flushed to distinct but harmonious tones of purple, and with one accusing voice they screamed, "You've shot the fox!"

Norah tried hastily to palliate Vladimir's misdeed in their eyes, but it is doubtful whether they heard her. The Major's fury clothed and reclothed itself in words as frantically as a woman up in town for one day's shopping tries on a succession of garments. He reviled and railed at fate and the general scheme of things, he pitied himself with a strong, deep pity too poignant for tears, he condemned every one with whom he had ever come in contact to endless and abnormal punishments. In fact, he conveyed the impression that if a destroying angel had been lent to him for a week it would have had very little time for private study. In the lulls of his outcry could be heard the querulous monotone of Mrs. Hoopington and the sharp staccato barking of the fox-terrier. Vladimir, who did not understand a tithe of what was being said, sat fondling a cigarette and repeating under his breath from time to time a vigorous

English adjective which he had long ago taken affectionately into his vocabulary. His mind strayed back to the youth in the old Russian folk-tale who shot an enchanted bird with dramatic results. Meanwhile, the Major, roaming round the hall like an imprisoned cyclone, had caught sight of and joyfully pounced on the telephone apparatus, and lost no time in ringing up the hunt secretary and announcing his resignation of the Mastership. A servant had by this time brought his horse round to the door, and in a few seconds Mrs. Hoopington's shrill monotone had the field to itself. But after the Major's display her best efforts at vocal violence missed their full effect; it was as though one had come straight out from a Wagner opera into a rather tame thunderstorm. Realising, perhaps, that her tirades were something of an anticlimax, Mrs. Hoopington broke suddenly into some rather necessary tears and marched out of the room, leaving behind her a silence almost as terrible as the turmoil which had preceded it.

" What shall I do with—*that*? " asked Vladimir at last.

" Bury it," said Norah.

" Just plain burial ? " said Vladimir, rather

relieved. He had almost expected that some of the local clergy would have insisted on being present, or that a salute might have to be fired over the grave.

And thus it came to pass that in the dusk of a November evening the Russian boy, murmuring a few of the prayers of his Church for luck, gave hasty but decent burial to a large polecat under the lilac trees at Hoopington.

THE STRATEGIST

MRS. JALLATT'S young people's parties were severely exclusive; it came cheaper that way, because you could ask fewer to them. Mrs. Jallatt didn't study cheapness, but somehow she generally attained it.

"There'll be about ten girls," speculated Rollo, as he drove to the function, "and I suppose four fellows, unless the Wrotsleys bring their cousin, which Heaven forbid. That would mean Jack and me against three of them."

Rollo and the Wrotsley brethren had maintained an undying feud almost from nursery days. They only met now and then in the holidays, and the meeting was usually tragic for whichever happened to have the fewest backers on hand. Rollo was counting to-night on the presence of a devoted and muscular partisan to hold an even balance. As he arrived he heard his prospective champion's sister apologising to the hostess for the unavoidable absence of her brother; a moment later he noted that the Wrotsleys *had* brought their cousin.

Two against three would have been exciting and possibly unpleasant; one against three promised to be about as amusing as a visit to a dentist. Rollo ordered his carriage for as early as was decently possible, and faced the company with a smile that he imagined the better sort of aristocrat would have worn when mounting to the guillotine.

"So glad you were able to come," said the elder Wrotsley heartily.

"Now, you children will like to play games, I suppose," said Mrs. Jallatt, by way of giving things a start, and as they were too well-bred to contradict her there only remained the question of what they were to play at.

"I know of a good game," said the elder Wrotsley innocently. "The fellows leave the room and think of a word; then they come back again, and the girls have to find out what the word is."

Rollo knew that game. He would have

suggested it himself if his faction had been in the majority.

"It doesn't promise to be very exciting," sniffed the superior Dolores Sneep as the boys filed out of the room. Rollo thought differently. He trusted to Providence that Wrotsley had nothing worse than knotted handkerchiefs at his disposal.

The word-choosers locked themselves in the library to ensure that their deliberations should not be interrupted. Providence turned out to be not even decently neutral; on a rack on the library wall were a dog-whip and a whalebone riding-switch. Rollo thought it criminal negligence to leave such weapons of precision lying about. He was given a choice of evils, and chose the dog-whip; the next minute or so he spent in wondering how he could have made such a stupid selection. Then they went back to the languidly expectant females.

"The word's 'camel,'" announced the Wrotsley cousin blunderingly.

"You stupid!" screamed the girls, "we've got to *guess* the word. Now you'll have to go back and think of another."

"Not for worlds," said Rollo; "I mean, the word isn't really camel; we were rotting.

Pretend it's dromedary ! " he whispered to the others.

" I heard them say 'dromedary'! I heard them. I don't care what you say; I heard them," squealed the odious Dolores. " With ears as long as hers one would hear anything," thought Rollo savagely.

" We shall have to go back, I suppose," said the elder Wrotsley resignedly.

The conclave locked itself once more into the library. " Look here, I'm not going through that dog-whip business again," protested Rollo.

" Certainly not, dear," said the elder Wrotsley; " we'll try the whalebone switch this time, and then you'll know which hurts most. It's only by personal experience that one finds out these things."

It was swiftly borne in upon Rollo that his earlier selection of the dog-whip had been a really sound one. The conclave gave his under-lip time to steady itself while it debated the choice of the necessary word. " Mustang " was no good, as half the girls wouldn't know what it meant; finally " quagga " was pitched on.

" You must come and sit down over here," chorused the investigating committee on their return; but Rollo was obdurate in insisting that the questioned person always stood up. On the whole, it was a relief when the game was ended and supper was announced.

Mrs. Jallatt did not stint her young guests, but the more expensive delicacies of her supper-table were never unnecessarily duplicated, and it was usually good policy to take what you wanted while it was still there. On this occasion she had provided sixteen peaches to "go round" among fourteen children; it was really not her fault that the two Wrotsleys and their cousin, foreseeing the long foodless drive home, had each quietly pocketed an extra peach, but it was distinctly trying for Dolores and the fat and good-natured Agnes Blaik to be left with one peach between them.

"I suppose we had better halve it," said Dolores sourly.

But Agnes was fat first and good-natured afterwards; those were her guiding principles in life. She was profuse in her sympathy for Dolores, but she hastily devoured the peach, explaining that it would spoil it to divide it; the juice ran out so.

"Now what would you all like to do?"

demanded Mrs. Jallatt by way of a diversion. "The professional conjurer whom I had engaged has failed me at the last moment. Can any of you recite?"

There were symptoms of a general panic. Dolores was known to recite "Locksley Hall" on the least provocation. There had been occasions when her opening line, "Comrades, leave me here a little," had been taken as a literal injunction by a large section of her hearers. There was a murmur of relief when Rollo hastily declared that he could do a few conjuring tricks. He had never done one in his life, but those two visits to the library had goaded him to unusual recklessness.

"You've seen conjuring chaps take coins and cards out of people," he announced; "well, I'm going to take more interesting things out of some of you. Mice, for instance."

"Not mice!"

A shrill protest rose, as he had foreseen, from the majority of his audience.

"Well, fruit, then."

The amended proposal was received with approval. Agnes positively beamed.

Without more ado Rollo made straight

for his trio of enemies, plunged his hand successively into their breast-pockets, and produced three peaches. There was no applause, but no amount of hand-clapping would have given the performer as much pleasure as the silence which greeted his coup.

"Of course, we were in the know," said the Wrotsley cousin lamely.

"That's done it," chuckled Rollo to himself.

"If they *had* been confederates they would have sworn they knew nothing about it," said Dolores, with piercing conviction.

"Do you know any more tricks?" asked Mrs. Jallatt hurriedly.

Rollo did not. He hinted that he might have changed the three peaches into something else, but Agnes had already converted one into girl-food, so nothing more could be done in that direction.

"I know a game," said the elder Wrotsley heavily, "where the fellows go out of the room, and think of some character in history; then they come back and act him, and the girls have to guess who it's meant for."

"I'm afraid I must be going," said Rollo to his hostess.

"Your carriage won't be here for another twenty minutes," said Mrs. Jallatt.

"It's such a fine evening I think I'll walk and meet it."

"It's raining rather steadily at present. You've just time to play that historical game."

"We haven't heard Dolores recite," said Rollo desperately; as soon as he had said it he realised his mistake. Confronted with the alternative of "Locksley Hall," public opinion declared unanimously for the history game.

Rollo played his last card. In an undertone meant apparently for the Wrotsley boy, but carefully pitched to reach Agnes, he observed—

"All right, old man; we'll go and finish those chocolates we left in the library."

"I think it's only fair that the girls should take their turn in going out," exclaimed Agnes briskly. She was great on fairness.

"Nonsense," said the others; "there are too many of us."

"Well, four of us can go. I'll be one of them."

And Agnes darted off towards the library, followed by three less eager damsels.

Rollo sank into a chair and smiled ever so faintly at the Wrotsleys, just a momentary baring of the teeth ; an otter, escaping from the fangs of the hounds into the safety of a deep pool, might have given a similar demonstration of its feelings.

From the library came the sound of moving furniture. Agnes was leaving nothing unturned in her quest for the mythical chocolates. And then came a more blessed sound, wheels crunching wet gravel.

" It has been a most enjoyable evening," said Rollo to his hostess.

CROSS CURRENTS

VANESSA PENNINGTON had a husband who was poor, with few extenuating circumstances, and an admirer who, though comfortably rich, was cumbered with a sense of honour. His wealth made him welcome in Vanessa's eyes, but his code of what was right impelled him to go away and forget her, or at the most to think of her in the intervals of doing a great many other things. And although Alaric Clyde loved Vanessa, and thought he should always go on loving her, he gradually and unconsciously allowed himself to be wooed and won by a more alluring mistress; he fancied that his continued shunning of the haunts of men was a self-imposed exile, but his heart was caught in the spell of the Wilderness, and the Wilderness was kind and beautiful to him. When one is young and strong and unfettered the wild earth can be very kind and very beautiful. Witness the legion of men who were once young and unfettered and now eat out their souls in dustbins, because, having erstwhile known and loved the Wilderness, they broke from her thrall and turned aside into beaten paths.

In the high waste places of the world Clyde roamed and hunted and dreamed, death-dealing and gracious as some god of Hellas, moving with his horses and servants and four-footed camp followers from one dwelling ground to another, a welcome guest among wild primitive village folk and nomads, a friend and slayer of the fleet, shy beasts around him. By the shores of misty upland lakes he shot the wild fowl that had winged their way to him across half the old world; beyond Bokhara he watched the wild Aryan horsemen at their gambols; watched, too, in some dim-lit tea-house one of those beautiful uncouth dances that one can never wholly forget; or, making a wide cast down to the valley of the Tigris, swam and rolled in its snow-cooled racing waters. Vanessa, meanwhile, in a Bayswater back street, was making out the weekly laundry list, attending bargain sales, and, in her more adventurous moments, trying new ways of cooking whiting.

Occasionally she went to bridge parties, where, if the play was not illuminating, at least one learned a great deal about the private life of some of the Royal and Imperial Houses. Vanessa, in a way, was glad that Clyde had done the proper thing. She had a strong natural bias towards respectability, though she would have preferred to have been respectable in smarter surroundings, where her example would have done more good. To be beyond reproach was one thing, but it would have been nicer to have been nearer to the Park.

And then of a sudden her regard for respectability and Clyde's sense of what was right were thrown on the scrap-heap of unnecessary things. They had been useful and highly important in their time, but the death of Vanessa's husband made them of no immediate moment.

The news of the altered condition of things followed Clyde with leisurely persistence from one place of call to another, and at last ran him to a standstill somewhere in the Orenburg Steppe. He would have found it exceedingly difficult to analyse his feelings on receipt of the tidings. The Fates had unexpectedly (and perhaps just a little officiously) removed an obstacle from his path. He supposed he was overjoyed, but he missed the feeling of elation which he had experienced some four months ago when he had bagged a snow-leopard with a lucky shot after a day's fruitless stalking. Of course he would go back and ask Vanessa to marry him, but he was determined on enforcing a condition: on no account would he desert his newer love. Vanessa would have to agree to come out into the Wilderness with him.

The lady hailed the return of her lover with even more relief than had been occasioned by his departure. The death of John Pennington had left his widow in circumstances which were more straitened than ever, and the Park had receded even from her notepaper, where it had long been retained as a courtesy title on the principle that addresses are given to us to conceal our whereabouts. Certainly she was more independent now than heretofore, but independence, which means so much to many women, was of little account to Vanessa, who came under the heading of the mere female. She made little ado about accepting Clyde's condition, and announced herself ready to

7

follow him to the end of the world; as the world was round she nourished a complacent idea that in the ordinary course of things one would find oneself in the neighbourhood of Hyde Park Corner sooner or later no matter how far afield one wandered.

East of Budapest her complacency began to filter away, and when she saw her husband treating the Black Sea with a familiarity which she had never been able to assume towards the English Channel, misgivings began to crowd in upon her. Adventures which would have presented an amusing and enticing aspect to a better-bred woman aroused in Vanessa only the twin sensations of fright and discomfort. Flies bit her, and she was persuaded that it was only sheer boredom that prevented camels from doing the same. Clyde did his best, and a very good best it was, to infuse something of the banquet into their prolonged desert picnics, but even snow-cooled Heidsieck lost its flavour when you were convinced that the dusky cupbearer who served it with such reverent elegance was only waiting a convenient opportunity to cut your throat. It was useless for Clyde to give Yussuf a character for devotion such as is rarely found in any Western servant. Vanessa was well enough educated to know that all dusky-skinned people take human life as unconcernedly as Bayswater folk take singing lessons.

And with a growing irritation and querulousness on her part came a further disenchantment, born of the inability of husband and wife to find a common ground of interest. The habits and migrations of the sand grouse, the folklore and customs of Tartars and Turkomans, the points of a Cossack pony — these were matters which evoked only a bored indifference in Vanessa. On the other hand, Clyde was not thrilled on being informed that the Queen of Spain detested mauve, or that a certain Royal duchess, for whose tastes he was never likely to be called on to cater, nursed a violent but perfectly respectable passion for beef olives.

Vanessa began to arrive at the conclusion that a husband who added a roving disposition to a settled income was a mixed blessing. It was one thing to go to the end of the world; it was quite another thing to make oneself at home there. Even respectability seemed to lose some of its virtue when one practised it in a tent.

Bored and disillusioned with the drift of her new life, Vanessa was undisguisedly glad when distraction offered itself in the person of Mr. Dobrinton, a chance acquaintance whom they had first run against in the primitive hostelry of a benighted Caucasian town. Dobrinton was elaborately British, in deference perhaps to the memory of his mother, who was said to have derived part of her origin from an English governess who had come to Lemberg a long way back in the last century. If you had called him Dobrinski when off his guard he would probably have responded readily enough; holding, no doubt, that the end crowns all, he had taken a slight liberty with the family patronymic. To look at, Mr. Dobrinton was not a very attractive specimen of masculine humanity, but in Vanessa's eyes he was a link with that civilisation which Clyde seemed so ready to ignore and forgo. He could sing "Yip-I-Addy" and spoke of several duchesses as if he knew them—in his more inspired moments almost as if they knew him. He even pointed out blemishes in the cuisine or cellar departments of some of the more august London restaurants, a species of Higher Criticism which was listened to by Vanessa in awe-stricken admiration. And, above all, he sympathised, at first discreetly, afterwards with more latitude, with her fretful discontent at Clyde's nomadic instincts. Business connected with oil-wells had brought Dobrinton to the neighbourhood of Baku; the pleasure of appealing to an appreciative female audience induced him to deflect his return journey so as to coincide a good deal with his new acquaintances' line of march. And while Clyde trafficked with Persian horse-dealers or hunted the wild grey pigs in their lairs and added to his notes on Central Asian game-fowl, Dobrinton and the lady discussed the ethics of desert respectability from points of view that showed a daily tendency to converge. And one evening Clyde dined alone, reading between the courses a long letter from Vanessa, justifying her action in flitting to more civilised lands with a more congenial companion.

It was distinctly evil luck for Vanessa, who really was thoroughly respectable at heart, that she and her lover should run into the hands of Kurdish brigands on the first day of their flight. To be mewed up in a squalid Kurdish village in close companionship with a man who was only your husband by adoption, and to have the attention of all Europe drawn to your plight, was about the least respectable thing that could happen. And there were international complications, which made things worse. "English lady and her husband, of foreign nationality, held by Kurdish brigands who demand ransom" had been the report of the nearest Consul. Although Dobrinton was British at heart, the other portions of him belonged to the Habsburgs, and though the Habsburgs took no great pride or pleasure in this particular unit of their wide and varied possessions, and would gladly have exchanged him for some interesting bird or mammal for the Schoenbrunn Park, the code of international dignity demanded that they should display a decent solicitude for his restoration. And while the Foreign Offices of the two countries were taking the usual steps to secure the release of their respective subjects a further horrible complication ensued. Clyde, following on the track of the fugitives, not with any special desire to overtake them, but with a dim feeling that it was expected of him, fell into the hands of the same community of brigands. Diplomacy, while anxious to do its best for a lady in misfortune, showed signs of becoming restive at this expansion of its task; as a frivolous young gentleman in Downing Street remarked, "Any husband of Mrs. Dobrinton's we shall be glad to extricate, but let us know how many there are of them." For a woman who valued respectability Vanessa really had no luck.

Meanwhile the situation of the captives was not free from embarrassment. When Clyde explained to the Kurdish headmen the nature of his relationship with the runaway couple they were gravely sympathetic, but vetoed any idea of summary vengeance, since the Habsburgs would be sure to insist on the delivery of Dobrinton alive, and in a reasonably undamaged condition. They did not object to Clyde administering a beating to his rival for half an hour every Monday and Thursday, but Dobrinton turned such a sickly green when he heard of this arrangement that the chief was obliged to withdraw the concession.

And so, in the cramped quarters of a mountain hut, the ill-assorted trio watched the insufferable hours crawl slowly by. Dobrinton was too frightened to be conversational, Vanessa was too mortified to open her lips, and Clyde was moodily silent.

The little Lemberg *négociant* plucked up heart once to give a quavering rendering of " Yip-I-Addy," but when he reached the statement " home was never like this " Vanessa tearfully begged him to stop. And silence fastened itself with growing insistence on the three captives who were so tragically herded together; thrice a day they drew near to one another to swallow the meal that had been prepared for them, like desert beasts meeting in mute suspended hostility at the drinking pool, and then drew back to resume the vigil of waiting.

Clyde was less carefully watched than the others. " Jealousy will keep him to the woman's side," thought his Kurdish captors. They did not know that his wilder, truer love was calling to him with a hundred voices from beyond the village bounds. And one evening, finding that he was not getting the attention to which he was entitled, Clyde slipped away down the mountain side and resumed his study of Central Asian game-fowl. The remaining captives were guarded henceforth with greater rigour, but Dobrinton at any rate scarcely regretted Clyde's departure.

The long arm, or perhaps one might better

say the long purse, of diplomacy at last effected the release of the prisoners, but the Habsburgs were never to enjoy the guerdon of their outlay. On the quay of the little Black Sea port, where the rescued pair came once more into contact with civilisation, Dobrinton was bitten by a dog which was assumed to be mad, though it may only have been indiscriminating. The victim did not wait for symptoms of rabies to declare themselves, but died forthwith of fright, and Vanessa made the homeward journey alone, conscious somehow of a sense of slightly restored respectability. Clyde, in the intervals of correcting the proofs of his book on the game-fowl of Central Asia, found time to press a divorce suit through the Courts, and as soon as possible hied him away to the congenial solitudes of the Gobi Desert to collect material for a work on the fauna of that region. Vanessa, by virtue perhaps of her earlier intimacy with the cooking rites of the whiting, obtained a place on the kitchen staff of a West End club. It was not brilliant, but at least it was within two minutes of the Park.

THE BAKER'S DOZEN

Characters—

MAJOR RICHARD DUMBARTON.
MRS. CAREWE.
MRS. PALY-PAGET.

Scene—Deck of eastward-bound steamer.
Major Dumbarton seated on deck-chair,
another chair by his side, with the name
"Mrs. Carewe" painted on it, a third near by.

(Enter R. Mrs. Carewe, seats herself
leisurely in her deck-chair, the Major affect-
ing to ignore her presence.)

Major (turning suddenly): Emily! After
all these years! This is fate!

Em.: Fate! Nothing of the sort; it's
only me. You men are always such fatalists.
I deferred my departure three whole weeks,
in order to come out in the same boat that I
saw you were travelling by. I bribed the
steward to put our chairs side by side in an

unfrequented corner, and I took enormous pains to be looking particularly attractive this morning, and then you say " This is fate." I *am* looking particularly attractive, am I not?

Maj.: More than ever. Time has only added a ripeness to your charms.

Em.: I knew you'd put it exactly in those words. The phraseology of love-making is awfully limited, isn't it? After all, the chief charm is in the fact of being made love to. You *are* making love to me, aren't you?

Maj.: Emily dearest, I had already begun making advances, even before you sat down here. I also bribed the steward to put our seats together in a secluded corner. "You may consider it done, sir," was his reply. That was immediately after breakfast.

Em.: How like a man to have his breakfast first. I attended to the seat business as soon as I left my cabin.

Maj.: Don't be unreasonable. It was only at breakfast that I discovered your blessed presence on the boat. I paid violent and unusual attention to a flapper all through the meal in order to make you jealous. She's probably in her cabin writing reams about me to a fellow-flapper at this very moment.

Em.: You needn't have taken all that trouble to make me jealous, Dickie. You did that years ago, when you married another woman.

Maj.: Well, you had gone and married another man—a widower, too, at that.

Em.: Well, there's no particular harm in marrying a widower, I suppose. I'm ready to do it again, if I meet a really nice one.

Maj.: Look here, Emily, it's not fair to go at that rate. You're a lap ahead of me the whole time. It's my place to propose to you; all you've got to do is to say "Yes."

Em.: Well, I've practically said it already, so we needn't dawdle over that part.

Maj.: Oh, well——

(They look at each other, then suddenly embrace with considerable energy.)

Maj.: We dead-heated it that time. (Suddenly jumping to his feet) Oh, d—— I'd forgotten!

Em.: Forgotten what?

Maj.: The children. I ought to have told you. Do you mind children?

Em.: Not in moderate quantities. How many have you got?

Maj. (counting hurriedly on his fingers): Five.

Em.: Five!

Maj. (anxiously): Is that too many?

Em.: It's rather a number. The worst of it is, I've some myself.

Maj.: Many?

Em.: Eight.

Maj.: Eight in six years! Oh, Emily!

Em.: Only four were my own. The other four were by my husband's first marriage. Still, that practically makes eight.

Maj.: And eight and five make thirteen. We can't start our married life with thirteen children ; it would be most unlucky. (Walks up and down in agitation.) Some way must be found out of this. If we could only bring them down to twelve. Thirteen is so horribly unlucky.

Em.: Isn't there some way by which we could part with one or two? Don't the French want more children? I've often seen articles about it in the *Figaro.*

Maj.: I fancy they want French children. Mine don't even speak French.

Em.: There's always a chance that one of them might turn out depraved and vicious, and then you could disown him. I've heard of that being done.

Maj.: But, good gracious, you've got to

educate him first. You can't expect a boy to be vicious till he's been to a good school.

Em.: Why couldn't he be naturally depraved. Lots of boys are.

Maj.: Only when they inherit it from depraved parents. You don't suppose there's any depravity in me, do you?

Em.: It sometimes skips a generation, you know. Weren't any of your family bad?

Maj.: There was an aunt who was never spoken of.

Em.: There you are!

Maj.: But one can't build too much on that. In mid-Victorian days they labelled all sorts of things as unspeakable that we should speak about quite tolerantly. I dare say this particular aunt had only married a Unitarian, or rode to hounds on both sides of her horse, or something of that sort. Anyhow, we can't wait indefinitely for one of the children to take after a doubtfully depraved great-aunt. Something else must be thought of.

Em.: Don't people ever adopt children from other families?

Maj.: I've heard of it being done by childless couples, and those sort of people——

Em.: Hush! Some one's coming. Who is it?

Maj.: Mrs. Paly-Paget.

Em.: The very person!

Maj.: What, to adopt a child? Hasn't she got any?

Em.: Only one miserable hen-baby.

Maj.: Let's sound her on the subject.

(Enter Mrs. Paly-Paget, R.)

Ah, good morning. Mrs. Paly-Paget. I was just wondering at breakfast where did we meet last?

Mrs. P.-P.: At the Criterion, wasn't it? (Drops into vacant chair.)

Maj.: At the Criterion, of course.

Mrs. P.-P.: I was dining with Lord and Lady Slugford. Charming people, but so mean. They took us afterwards to the Velodrome, to see some dancer interpreting Mendelssohn's "songs without clothes." We were all packed up in a little box near the roof, and you may imagine how hot it was. It was like a Turkish bath. And, of course, one couldn't see anything.

Maj.: Then it was not like a Turkish bath.

Mrs. P.-P.: Major!

Em.: We were just talking of you when you joined us.

Mrs. P.-P.: Really! Nothing very dreadful, I hope.

Em.: Oh dear, no! It's too early on the voyage for that sort of thing. We were feeling rather sorry for you.

Mrs. P.-P.: Sorry for me? Whatever for?

Maj.: Your childless hearth and all that, you know. No little pattering feet.

Mrs. P.-P.: Major! How dare you? I've got my little girl, I suppose you know. Her feet can patter as well as other children's.

Maj.: Only one pair of feet.

Mrs. P.-P.: Certainly. My child isn't a centipede. Considering the way they move us about in those horrid jungle stations, without a decent bungalow to set one's foot in, I consider I've got a heartless child, rather than a childless hearth. Thank you for your sympathy all the same. I dare say it was well meant. Impertinence often is.

Em: Dear Mrs. Paly-Paget, we were only feeling sorry for your sweet little girl when she grows older, you know, No little brothers and sisters to play with.

Mrs. P.-P.: Mrs. Carewe, this conversation strikes me as being indelicate, to say the least of it. I've only been married two and a half years, and my family is naturally a small one.

Maj.: Isn't it rather an exaggeration to talk of one little female child as a family? A family suggests numbers.

Mrs. P.-P.: Really, Major, your language is extraordinary. I dare say I've only got a little female child, as you call it, at present——

Maj.: Oh, it won't change into a boy later on, if that's what you're counting on. Take our word for it; we've had so much more experience in these affairs than you have. Once a female, always a female. Nature is not infallible, but she always abides by her mistakes.

Mrs. P.-P. (rising): Major Dumbarton, these boats are uncomfortably small, but I trust we shall find ample accommodation for avoiding each other's society during the rest of the voyage. The same wish applies to you, Mrs. Carewe.

(Exit Mrs. Paly-Paget, L.)

Maj.: What an unnatural mother! (Sinks into chair.)

Em.: I wouldn't trust a child with any one who had a temper like hers. Oh, Dickie, why did you go and have such a large family?

8

You always said you wanted me to be the mother of your children.

Maj.: I wasn't going to wait while you were founding and fostering dynasties in other directions. Why you couldn't be content to have children of your own, without collecting them like batches of postage stamps I can't think. The idea of marrying a man with four children !

Em.: Well, you're asking me to marry one with five.

Maj.: Five ! (Springing to his feet) Did I say five ?

Em.: You certainly said five.

Maj.: Oh, Emily, supposing I've miscounted them ! Listen now, keep count with me. Richard—that's after me, of course.

Em.: One.

Maj.: Albert-Victor—that must have been in Coronation year.

Em.: Two !

Maj.: Maud. She's called after——

Em.: Never mind who's she's called after. Three !

Maj.: And Gerald.

Em.: Four !

Maj.: That's the lot.

Em.: Are you sure ?

Maj.: I swear that's the lot.   I must have counted Albert-Victor as two.

Em.: Richard!

Maj.: Emily!

(They embrace.)

THE MOUSE

THEODORIC VOLER had been
brought up, from infancy to the
confines of middle age, by a fond mother
whose chief solicitude had been to keep him
screened from what she called the coarser
realities of life. When she died she left
Theodoric alone in a world that was as real
as ever, and a good deal coarser than he
considered it had any need to be. To a
man of his temperament and upbringing
even a simple railway journey was crammed
with petty annoyances and minor discords,
and as he settled himself down in a second-
class compartment one September morning
he was conscious of ruffled feelings and
general mental discomposure. He had been
staying at a country vicarage, the inmates
of which had been certainly neither brutal
nor bacchanalian, but their supervision of
the domestic establishment had been of that

lax order which invites disaster. The pony
carriage that was to take him to the station
had never been properly ordered, and when
the moment for his departure drew near
the handy-man who should have produced
the required article was nowhere to be
found. In this emergency Theodoric, to
his mute but very intense disgust, found
himself obliged to collaborate with the vicar's
daughter in the task of harnessing the pony,
which necessitated groping about in an ill-
lighted outhouse called a stable, and smelling
very like one—except in patches where it
smelt of mice. Without being actually
afraid of mice, Theodoric classed them
among the coarser incidents of life, and
considered that Providence, with a little
exercise of moral courage, might long ago
have recognised that they were not indis-
pensable, and have withdrawn them from
circulation. As the train glided out of the
station Theodoric's nervous imagination
accused himself of exhaling a weak odour
of stable-yard, and possibly of displaying a
mouldy straw or two on his usually well-
brushed garments. Fortunately the only
other occupant of the compartment, a lady
of about the same age as himself, seemed

inclined for slumber rather than scrutiny;
the train was not due to stop till the terminus
was reached, in about an hour's time, and
the carriage was of the old-fashioned sort,
that held no communication with a corridor,
therefore no further travelling companions
were likely to intrude on Theodoric's semi-
privacy. And yet the train had scarcely
attained its normal speed before he became
reluctantly but vividly aware that he was
not alone with the slumbering lady; he was
not even alone in his own clothes. A warm,
creeping movement over his flesh betrayed
the unwelcome and highly resented presence,
unseen but poignant, of a strayed mouse,
that had evidently dashed into its present
retreat during the episode of the pony
harnessing. Furtive stamps and shakes and
wildly directed pinches failed to dislodge
the intruder, whose motto, indeed, seemed to
be Excelsior; and the lawful occupant of
the clothes lay back against the cushions
and endeavoured rapidly to evolve some
means for putting an end to the dual owner-
ship. It was unthinkable that he should
continue for the space of a whole hour in
the horrible position of a Rowton House
for vagrant mice (already his imagination

had at least doubled the numbers of the alien invasion). On the other hand, nothing less drastic than partial disrobing would ease him of his tormentor, and to undress in the presence of a lady, even for so laudable a purpose, was an idea that made his eartips tingle in a blush of abject shame. He had never been able to bring himself even to the mild exposure of open-work socks in the presence of the fair sex. And yet—the lady in this case was to all appearances soundly and securely asleep; the mouse, on the other hand, seemed to be trying to crowd a Wanderjahr into a few strenuous minutes. If there is any truth in the theory of transmigration, this particular mouse must certainly have been in a former state a member of the Alpine Club. Sometimes in its eagerness it lost its footing and slipped for half an inch or so; and then, in fright, or more probably temper, it bit. Theodoric was goaded into the most audacious undertaking of his life. Crimsoning to the hue of a beetroot and keeping an agonised watch on his slumbering fellow-traveller, he swiftly and noiselessly secured the ends of his railway-rug to the racks on either side of the carriage, so that a substantial curtain hung athwart the compartment. In the narrow dressing-room that he had thus improvised he proceeded with violent haste to extricate himself partially and the mouse entirely from the surrounding casings of tweed and half-wool. As the unravelled mouse gave a wild leap to the floor, the rug, slipping its fastening at either end, also came down with a heart-curdling flop, and almost simultaneously the awakened sleeper opened her eyes. With a movement almost quicker than the mouse's, Theodoric pounced on the rug, and hauled its ample folds chin-high over his dismantled person as he collapsed into the further corner of the carriage. The blood raced and beat in the veins of his neck and forehead, while he waited dumbly for the communication-cord to be pulled. The lady, however, contented herself with a silent stare at her strangely muffled companion. How much had she seen, Theodoric queried to himself, and in any case what on earth must she think of his present posture?

" I think I have caught a chill," he ventured desperately.

" Really, I'm sorry," she replied. " I was just going to ask you if you would open this window."

" I fancy it's malaria," he added, his teeth chattering slightly, as much from fright as from a desire to support his theory.

" I've got some brandy in my hold-all, if you'll kindly reach it down for me," said his companion.

" Not for worlds—I mean, I never take anything for it," he assured her earnestly.

" I suppose you caught it in the Tropics ? "

Theodoric, whose acquaintance with the Tropics was limited to an annual present of a chest of tea from an uncle in Ceylon, felt that even the malaria was slipping from him. Would it be possible, he wondered, to disclose the real state of affairs to her in small instalments ?

" Are you afraid of mice ? " he ventured, growing, if possible, more scarlet in the face.

" Not unless they came in quantities, like those that ate up Bishop Hatto. Why do you ask ? "

" I had one crawling inside my clothes just now," said Theodoric in a voice that hardly seemed his own. " It was a most awkward situation."

" It must have been, if you wear your clothes at all tight," she observed ; " but mice have strange ideas of comfort."

"I had to get rid of it while you were asleep," he continued ; then, with a gulp, he added, "it was getting rid of it that brought me to—to this."

"Surely leaving off one small mouse wouldn't bring on a chill," she exclaimed, with a levity that Theodoric accounted abominable.

Evidently she had detected something of his predicament, and was enjoying his confusion. All the blood in his body seemed to have mobilised in one concentrated blush, and an agony of abasement, worse than a myriad mice, crept up and down over his soul. And then, as reflection began to assert itself, sheer terror took the place of humiliation. With every minute that passed the train was rushing nearer to the crowded and bustling terminus where dozens of prying eyes would be exchanged for the one paralysing pair that watched him from the further corner of the carriage. There was one slender despairing chance, which the next few minutes must decide. His fellow-traveller might relapse into a blessed slumber. But as the minutes throbbed by that chance ebbed away. The furtive glance which Theodoric stole at her from time

to time disclosed only an unwinking wake-
fulness.

"I think we must be getting near now,"
she presently observed.

Theodoric had already noted with growing
terror the recurring stacks of small, ugly
dwellings that heralded the journey's end.
The words acted as a signal. Like a hunted
beast breaking cover and dashing madly towards some other haven of momentary safety
he threw aside his rug, and struggled frantically into his dishevelled garments. He was
conscious of dull surburban stations racing
past the window, of a choking, hammering
sensation in his throat and heart, and of an
icy silence in that corner towards which he
dared not look. Then as he sank back in his
seat, clothed and almost delirious, the train
slowed down to a final crawl, and the woman
spoke.

"Would you be so kind," she asked, "as to
get me a porter to put me into a cab? It's
a shame to trouble you when you're feeling
unwell, but being blind makes one so helpless
at a railway station."